THIS IS GRACE
I Saw the Hand of God

VENETIA ZANNETTIS

Venetia Zannettis

Email: Venetia.VenetiaZ@gmail.com
Social Media: Venetia Zannettis Ministries

Scripture quotations taken from the New King James Version®. Copyright © 1982 by Thomas Nelson. Used by permission. All rights reserved.

Scripture quotations taken from The Holy Bible, New International Version® NIV® Copyright © 1973 1978 1984 2011 by Biblica, Inc. ™ Used by permission. All rights reserved worldwide.

TABLE OF CONTENTS

Preface 7

Have You Met My Lord? 9
Dying Teen to Jesus 14
Sixteen and Suicidal..18
Saved From Suicide, Addiction, and Schizophrenia 22
I Found Hope and Peace in Jesus............................30
Twenty-Year-Old Homeless Crackhead.....................35
Shot Five Times and Left for Dead 40
I Met Jesus in the Mountains 45
Jesus Came to Me in Solitary Confinement..............48
I Found Love After Stepfather's Sexual Abuse..........53
I Can Do All Through Christ 58
Hindu Leader to Jesus Christ 61
I Saw the Light of Christ 67
Healed From HIV 71
I Never Knew God 76
From Islam to Jesus 82
When a Child's Soul Gets Shattered Through Abuse 89
I Saw the Hand of God 92
The Spirit of this World...98
Jesus Christ Our Saviour 105
The Kingdom of God 113
Your Inheritance in Christ 119
God Is Looking for Committed Vessels...................123
The Choice of Life and Death 126

About Info 131

PREFACE

"Bless the LORD, O my soul;
And all that is within me, bless His holy name!
Bless the LORD, O my soul,
And forget not all His benefits:
Who forgives all your iniquities,
Who heals all your diseases,
Who redeems your life from destruction,
Who crowns you with lovingkindness and tender mercies,
Who satisfies your mouth with good things,
So that your youth is renewed like the eagle's.
The LORD executes righteousness
And justice for all who are oppressed.
He made known His ways to Moses,
His acts to the children of Israel.
The LORD is merciful and gracious,
Slow to anger, and abounding in mercy"

(Psalm 103:1-8 NKJV).

For personal reasons, the names mentioned in this book have been altered.

HAVE YOU MET MY LORD?

Have you met my Lord, Jesus Christ?

He raised the dead
He turned water into wine
He parted the Red Sea
He walked on water
He healed the lepers
He broke the chains of bondage and set the captives free
He made the blind see
He made the cripple walk
He cast out a legion of demons
He healed the sick
He paid taxes out of the mouth of a fish
He calmed the storm
He fed 5,000 people with five loaves of bread and two fish
He resurrected from the dead and is alive today
He is sitting at the right hand of God the Father today
He is still performing miracles to this day

Jesus is the living Word of God. He is alive and here today. Do you have a relationship with Jesus? Do you know Him as your Saviour?

Although Jesus is the miracle worker, wickedness and evil still exist; and corruption is growing, because man chooses to reject Him. People are living in sin, and in rebellion against God; and for this, man is dying in his evil ways. Living in sin means taking a sinful course of life. It is the situation in which one's life is perpetually sinful, or the condition in which one's deeds do not conform to the Word of God. The sin in the world is due to rejecting God and choosing to live a self-appetizing, self-centered, and self-obsessed life. It is a selfish life that puts self before God. Understand that a world full of selfish people means greed, pride, revenge, murder, and all that is not of God – this is sin.

Due to sin, humankind lives in a state of miserable experiences where millions of lost souls around the globe are ever so helpless, never given a chance to experience love. Both their mind and body live in torment – they become the walking dead, thinking they live while spiritually dead. These are the consequence of turning away from God and living in sin.

Understand that sin is the work of the devil, which means that most of humanity is ignorantly following in the ways of Satan. They get held captive to sin by the spiritual forces of evil operating in this world. Worldwide, people are perishing in the prison of darkness, under its power, held captive by Satan at his will. The destruction on this earth is indeed spiritual, not physical. Our spiritual enemies are demonic armies attacking people. The evil happening in the world is not God tormenting humankind. The spiritual force of evil entities afflicts society due to man's sinful choices and rebellion against God. God has given man free will to choose between sin and righteousness, and man chooses sin over purity. Thus, the corruption we see in the world is man suffering the consequences of his sinful choices. Humanity's works defile them. They seek relief but find none because all sin leads to separation from God, destruction, and death.

"For the wages of sin is death" (Romans 6:23 NKJV).

There are terrible consequences to going against how God designed us to live. Yet regardless of the pain, man continues to sin, because the sinful life superficially feels good. But know this: It's only a short-lived feel-good bait that lures man deeper into wickedness, eventually throwing many into anxiety, deep depression, insanity, schizophrenia, and even suicide.

Humankind cannot keep soundness of mind, for the severity of sadness, hopelessness, and terror torments them day and night. These are the consequences of sin. Due to desperation, people are reaching out to worldly solutions for relief; but in a world designed to deceive, there is no relief. As desperation rises, standards fall, knocking man deeper into sin and wickedness.

People are dying in a dying world and have no idea how to handle it. Let me tell you this: "Jesus is the only One who can set man free." The only way to get protected from this wicked and darkened world is through Jesus Christ.

"The reason the Son of God appeared was to destroy the devil's work" (1 John 3:8 NIV).

Jesus came to destroy the devil's works. A massive part of Christ's ministry was healing the sick and casting out demonic spirits. That's how He set people free, and all He encountered got miraculously healed and liberated. The only way to defeat the enemy is through Jesus Christ.

Jesus said, *"The Spirit of the Lord God is upon Me, because the Lord has anointed Me to preach good tidings to the poor; He has sent Me to heal the brokenhearted, to proclaim liberty to the captives, and the opening of the prison to those who are bound" (Isaiah 61:1 NKJV).*

Jesus is the Light Who stepped down from heaven into this darkened world to set man free from corruption and sin. Because the punishment of sin is death, Jesus bore our sins on His body, making the great exchange: our sins for His righteousness, our death for a new life in Him. Thus He removed our guilt and freed us from the punishment of corruption.

"He was wounded for our transgressions, He was bruised for our iniquities; the chastisement for our peace was upon Him, and by His stripes we are healed" (Isaiah 53:5 NKJV).

Reader, Jesus suffered in our place that we may be set free. He took the punishment for our sins, took our place, took on our pain, and took our punishment. He was the sacrificial lamb who gave His life in exchange for ours, whereby he made our peace and reconciliation with God. Understand that sin is a disease that affects all men; but by the blood of Christ, all sin got forgiven, and the condition of sin healed.

"Surely He has borne our griefs and carried our sorrows; yet we esteemed Him stricken, smitten by God, and afflicted" (Isaiah 53:4 NKJV).

We are free because Jesus bought our freedom with His blood. Thus, we got healed by the stripes on His back from the scourging inflicted on Him. Christ heals by taking the sicknesses of humanity upon Himself. He liberates by taking the bondage of humankind upon Himself. He makes innocent by taking the guilt of humanity upon Himself. Man is free from sin and corruption through Christ's crucifixion on the cross. All have been healed and liberated by the suffering of Jesus Christ. Even death and the grave could not defeat Him, for Jesus rose from the dead on the third day with all power in His hand.

Thus, *"Whoever calls on the name of the Lord shall be saved" (Romans 10:13 NKJV).*

God will give salvation, deliverance, healing, forgiveness, and reconciliation with God to all who call on Jesus. Those who put their faith in Christ and His sacrifice on the cross will get saved, but those who reject Him will face the wrath of God. Reader, there is no other way to obtain heaven but through Jesus Christ. Denying the truth of the finished work on the cross is rejecting life itself.

Call upon the Name of the Lord and be saved. God will do such an excellent job of cleaning you up after all the mess you got yourself into that even the broken people who look at you will think you have never been through anything. Like all believers in Christ, we have been through much, but Jesus cleans us well.

There are those of you sitting at home reading this book, thinking you are the worst person and in the worst position. You're looking at your bankruptcy, your family, shame, guilt, fear, and thinking there's no one else like you, or no one else in such a bad position. Maybe you look at people walking with Christ and believe they've never been through anything; so how can they know anything? But little do you know that the people walking with Christ have also walked through darkness and pain, just like you; but the grace of God carried them through the whole way. And they are here today only by the grace of God. By God's grace, I am one of those who got carried from darkness to freedom. I encourage you to read the testimonies below if you want proof of Jesus' ability to save, heal, and deliver.

DYING TEEN TO JESUS

Tony's Story
I was raised in an abusive Mormon household. My life was boring and lifeless, as was the Mormon religion I followed. Due to my abusive dad, I had emotional, behavioural, and developmental problems. I was diagnosed with bipolar, borderline personality disorder, autism, and PTSD. At 13, I began feeling completely useless, worthless, and powerless. I was losing control of my thoughts and emotions. In the hope of gaining back power, I started experimenting with the occult, Satanism, and Wicca. I got heavily into witchcraft, and my life went from bad to worse. I suffered many demonic attacks.

Then when I was 16, I came out to my parents as bisexual. They kicked me out of the house. I was heartbroken and scared, thinking I would die alone on the street. Walking the streets, I fell into a depressive state. Then one day, while street walking, my foot was run over by a land rover. I was on crutches for weeks. One afternoon, a random Christian woman that I did not know asked to pray for my speedy recovery. I accepted. She prayed in the Name of Jesus, and by the following day, I was fully healed and had no need of the crutches. Regardless of the miracle, I still denied Christ.

Then one day, I felt a need to go to church. At church, I had an inner urge to remove my satanic pentagram necklace, so I took it off. I started having thoughts of converting from satanism to Christianity. I asked God into my heart and felt His Holy Spirit in me. I obtained a Bible and a cross necklace and aimed to learn everything I could about the gospel.

I attended church every week, and then I got baptized. It was the most beautiful experience of my life. My journey with Christ has been completely life-changing. I am no longer homeless, I no longer struggle with depression, homosexuality, or any other disorder I mentioned, and all demonic attacks have ceased. Jesus saved me.
– Tony

Reader, allow me to explain the spiritual side of young Tony's life. We see multiple violations of God's principles; thus, spiritual doors opened, and forces of evil entered his life. For example, due to Tony's upbringing, he was caught up in a religion without God: Mormonism. When people seek religion through unbiblical doctrine, they find the devil, because he's waiting there to feed them lies. God didn't tell Tony to mix with unbiblical teachings.

The Bible says, *"Whoever transgresses and does not abide in the doctrine of Christ does not have God. He who abides in the doctrine of Christ has both the Father and the Son. If anyone comes to you and does not bring this doctrine, do not receive him into your house nor greet him; for he who greets him shares in his evil deeds"* (2 John 1:9-11 NKJV).

The Bible tells us that unbiblical teachings are a transgression and evil deeds. Please understand that false religions bring demonic problems. These wicked issues are first commandment violations:

"You shall have no other gods before Me" (Exodus 20:3 NKJV).

When God's spiritual principles get violated through false religions and fake gods, we start to see demonic manifestations, as in the case of Tony's household: abusive family, bipolar, PTSD, autism, etc. Note that the evil will keep escalating because the devil is given a foothold.

Secondly, Tony got caught up in ungodly spirituality: occult, Satanism, and Wicca. Know this: spirituality without God brings curses. God didn't tell Tony to abandon His Holy Word and follow Satan's occult practices. That was Tony's choice.

Instead, Jesus said, *"You shall love the Lord your God with all your heart, with all your soul, and with all your mind"* (Matthew 22:37 NKJV).

Such Satanic practices are crawling with demons who deceive its victims into destructive paths, bringing confusion, depression, and sometimes suicide. Once these demons are in a person's life, they will inflict all sorts of feelings on their victim: feelings of worthlessness, discouragement, powerlessness, and as we see in the life of young Tony, identity disorder (bisexuality, for example). Bisexuality is not normal. It's not from God, for God created man and woman in His perfect image.

"God created man in His own image; in the image of God He created him; male and female He created them" (Genesis 1:27 NKJV).

God does not make mistakes with genders, which means that gender dysphoria is a demonic attack on the individual. The more people play in the devil's playground, experimenting with genders, the more they give the devil a foothold. God did not tell mankind to experiment with genders; that is man's sinful choice.

The Bible warns, *"You shall not lie with a male as with a woman. It is an abomination" (Leviticus 18:22 NKJV).*

And so, once people start opening demonic doors through disobedience and rebellion against God, these demons will come in and cause havoc. Moreover, those demons will continue to pave the way for the next unclean spirit to come into the victim's life. Before we know it, we are drowning in chronic depression, anxiety, fear, and health issues - typical signs of demonic affliction and oppression. And life will continue to worsen for the individual until Jesus comes in as their personal Saviour.

Notice that it was not until a woman of God (sent by God) stepped in and prayed for Tony that things started to shift in his life. Tony did his part by accepting prayer from the woman of God rather than rejecting prayer. By accepting, Tony said, "I need help; I want change." In other words, he willingly reached out to God, rejecting his sinful ways. Then the removal of his satanic necklace followed. Tony had a choice: His old life or God? He chose God, allowing Christ to come into his heart. Thus, he was saved and filled with the Holy Spirit, and the improvements to his life began. Notice that once Jesus was in, everything about Tony's life changed. That's the power of Jesus Christ. And so, if you are going through a similar issue as young Tony, know that God is faithful to forgive and forget, and welcome you into His loving embrace. Turn to Him.

"Good and upright is the Lord; therefore He teaches sinners in the way. The humble He guides in justice, and the humble He teaches His way. All the paths of the Lord are mercy and truth, to such as keep His covenant and His testimonies. For Your name's sake, O Lord, pardon my iniquity, for it is great" (Psalm 25:8-11 NKJV).

SIXTEEN AND SUICIDAL

Pamela's Story
I've dealt with an abusive brother who mentally and physically abused my parents and me. I've been through depression, self-harm, and marijuana addiction because of the abuse. Suicide was constantly on my mind. I even planned out my death. I thought I would never be okay, and my only escape was to kill myself. I was wrong.

At 15, I met a guy with whom I fell in love, and we planned on getting married. But then, one day, he found a new girl, and I was the girl on the side for a whole year. Life was miserable for me. I could not function. I planned on committing suicide, but something inside me told me to move on and forget about him. I did. Dealing with my abusive brother, who often got aggressive with my parents, depression overcame me, and I started smoking marijuana. I couldn't go a day without it.

My life was miserable. One day, I decided to try the church, for until then, I was an atheist and was against the church. At church, I started praying for my family. For the first time in my life, I got down on my knees, and with tears in my eyes, I asked God to help me. God heard my prayer, and the change was instant.

Today my depression is gone, and I haven't self-harmed ever since. I quit smoking marijuana, and I got baptized. I found peace in God. God continues to hear every prayer. He is faithful. My life is no longer pointless but meaningful. Thank you, Jesus.
-Pamela Reif

Reader, allow me to explain the spiritual side of Pamela's case. Within her family, we see multiple violations of God's spiritual principles: parent–child relationship to be exact. For example, children are a precious gift from God. Parents are responsible for caring for them, protecting them, and especially keeping them covered in prayer. The parent is the head of the child, just as Christ is the head of the parent. And as Christ protects the parent, the parent is to protect the child.

"Fathers, do not provoke your children to anger, but bring them up in the discipline and instruction of the Lord" (Ephesians 6:4 NKJV).

Sadly, if the parent does not have Christ as the head of the household, then the parent cannot discipline the child in the instruction of the Lord. This household and upbringing of the child is sure to operate under some other force; thus, demonic problems will follow, as we see in Pamela's case.

For this reason, *"Train up a child in the way he should go; even when he is old he will not depart from it" (Proverbs 22:6 NKJV).*

Unfortunately, Pamela grew up in an atheist family, where God and His ways got rejected. Understand that when God's sovereignty is not recognized, God's Kingdom is not yet come. Therefore, any such household operates under dark power, as we see in Pamela's home with her atheist parents, abusive brother, mental/ emotional issues, etc.

As demons tend to pave the way for the next unclean spirit to come into our lives, the path got paved for depression, self-harm, and addiction to enter Pamela's life. Very quickly, suicidal thoughts followed. Once the enemy had settled in her life, more demons of a different nature started showing up, such as of a sexual nature – fornication. Fornication is another severe violation of God's laws. God does not tell us to fornicate; He speaks against it.

*"Do you not know that the unrighteous will not inherit the kingdom of God? Do not be deceived. Neither **fornicators**, nor idolaters, nor adulterers, nor homosexuals, nor sodomites, nor thieves, nor covetous, nor drunkards, nor revilers, nor extortioners will inherit the kingdom of God. And such were some of you" (1 Corinthians 6:9-11 NKJV).*

Sex outside of marriage is called fornication, and it is sin. And when we violate God's principles, we will suffer the consequences of our transgressions. We must understand that sexual sin is a serious matter, and one should not take it lightly.

"Marriage is honorable among all, and the bed undefiled; but fornicators and adulterers God will judge" (Hebrews 13:4 NKJV).

We can't expect an intimate relationship filled with peace and unconditional love if we violate God's principles. When we eat from the forbidden tree, our sexual relationship is sure to go through pressure, fear, anxiety, rejection, jealousy, dissatisfaction, and more. When we transgress against God, we will suffer the consequences of our sinful choices. Thus, in Pamela's case, rejection from her boyfriend followed, then manipulation, filling Pamela with misery.

However, even in all her mess, the Holy Spirit faithfully led her: 'Let go and move on." Although Pamela thought it was her intuition nudging her to move on, it was the Holy Spirit. The Spirit of the Lord is continuously nudging people of all races and walks of life to turn to Christ and be saved. God has multiple ways of leading us to Christ: through a minister of Christ, a God-sent vision, Christ appearing in person, Scripture, etc. At the same time, God gives us all free will to accept or reject Christ.

Notice that it was not until Pamela decided to go to church, get down on her knees and pray, asking God for help, did her life start to change. God heard her cry and stepped in.

"Whoever calls on the name of the Lord shall be saved" (Romans 10:13 NKJV).

Once Jesus came in, change followed, salvation and freedom come to her. Pamela was healed of all old wounds and found peace in Christ.

"For He Himself is our peace" (Ephesians 2:14 NKJV).

Christ is our peace. There is no peace without Him. Pamela's life now has meaning because God gave her life meaning. Understand that we lose meaning and purpose when we rebel and reject God. Reader, if you are going through the same issue as Pamela, remember:

"I love the Lord, because He has heard my voice and my supplications. Because He has inclined His ear to me, therefore I will call upon Him as long as I live. The pains of death surrounded me, and the pangs of Sheol laid hold of me; I found trouble and sorrow. Then I called upon the name of the Lord: "O Lord, I implore You, deliver my soul!" Gracious is the Lord, and righteous; yes, our God is merciful. The Lord preserves the simple; I was brought low, and He saved me. Return to your rest, O my soul, for the Lord has dealt bountifully with you. For You have delivered my soul from death, my eyes from tears, and my feet from falling. I will walk before the Lord in the land of the living" (Psalm 116:1-9 NKJV).

SAVED FROM SUICIDE, ADDICTION, AND SCHIZOPHRENIA

Julie's Story
Ever since I can remember, I have always wanted to die. I never experienced what it was like to want to live. Although I loved the idea of God as a little girl, I never knew Him personally. Almost everyone in my family had battled severe drug addiction and mental health problems, including me.

One night, I overdosed. I felt my life leaving me. My heart was racing out of my chest, and I began to black out. The next thing I remember was the sound of people praying around me. I didn't know these people, but I could feel them laying their hands on me while praying for me. After I regained consciousness, my heart was beating normally, and I could breathe again. It was as though the overdose hadn't happened.

The following day, I called my grandmother, who told me about a close friend, Jack, who was in prison. Jack encountered Jesus in prison and gave his life to Him. My grandmother told me that the previous night (the night I overdosed), Jack and all his prayer friends in prison were interceding to God for me. The Holy Spirit told them what to pray and for whom to pray. I started crying. Immediately, I knew who these people were that prayed over me and laid hands on me during my overdose.

Regardless of their prayers that saved my life, I could not break the addiction. I had lived as a prisoner inside my mind for many years, and addiction was all I knew. No rehab was able to break the habit. I was trapped. I began to sink low in complete despair. I was going to commit suicide. I could not bear living that way any longer. So, I made a passionate and desperate plea to God in the privacy of my bedroom. I prayed and asked Him to free me from the stronghold of drug addiction. I challenged God and told Him, "God, You have until Sunday to deliver me; otherwise, I will kill myself. Your Word says

You died for my addiction. If this is true, all I should do is tell You that I do not want it anymore, and it should be gone. So, God, I don't want it anymore." With tears in my eyes, I surrendered my addiction to Him and let Him take it off me. I knew immediately that the stronghold had broken, and I was free.

Only my mental health problems remained. I had tried multiple anti-psychotic pills, and none of them could cure me. Diagnosed with bipolar and then schizophrenia, I refused even to leave the house anymore. And that was when I made another passionate plea to God. "God, get this spirit of suicide and depression and mental illness off me."

Then God spoke, saying, "Praise Me because the devil cannot stand in the praises of God." So, I began praising God. I praised Him for three days ongoing. Throughout the three days, I would feel the heaviness lift bit by bit. God was delivering me. The following day when I awoke, I put on a worship song that I usually hated listening to, and the spirit of suicide and depression left me instantly.

Suddenly, I could hear God. My mind was clear. I was ok. That was the end of suicidal thoughts, depression, thoughts of murder, and all such things. God saved me. All the chains that had held me captive shattered, the prison doors flew wide open, and I was set free. Hallelujah, praise God!

That is what Jesus Christ, my Saviour did for me, and He will do it for you if you let Him. Jesus is the only One who can save, heal, and deliver you.
-Julie Thomas

Reader, in the spiritual realm, Julie had generational issues passed on from one age to the next. The spirit of addiction and infirmity was generational, for Julie testified that almost everyone in her family battled severe drug addiction and mental health problems.

"I, the Lord your God, am a jealous God, visiting the iniquity of the fathers upon the children to the third and fourth generations of those who hate Him" (Deuteronomy 5:9 NKJV).

Just as a necklace gets passed down in a family for generations, so can curses, demons, diseases, addiction, and more. That is not to say that children get punished for the sins of their fathers or that God punishes entire families for the sin of one of their members. Certainly not! God is not an unjust God.

"The son shall not bear the guilt of the father, nor the father bear the guilt of the son. The righteousness of the righteous shall be upon himself, and the wickedness of the wicked shall be upon himself" (Ezekiel 18: 20 NKJV).

In other words, each person suffers the consequences for their sins.

"He will render to each one according to his works" (Romans 2:6 NKJV).

Each person will be responsible for their choices. Understand that this is not some mystical curse God placed on children because of their fathers' deeds. Instead, the curses of our ancestors are passed down in a family for generations. For this reason, a dad's sins are often the same ones his children struggle with. Only when Jesus comes in does the chain break, for Jesus is the only One who cancelled all curses at the cross of Calvary.

As the curse passes from generation to generation, the individual has free will to choose Christ, or to continue living in family sin, thus extending the curse. The choice is ours, for God has given us free will. If we continue the family sin, we partake in the curse. If we choose Christ over the family sin, the curse gets broken, and we are free through Christ alone. You get to choose what you will set into motion: curses or blessings.

For instance, it is evident that, after drinking poison, death will follow. That's not because God killed you, but because death is in the poison. Likewise, when living in sin, curses follow. That's not because God cursed you, but because the curse is within sin. Each person lives the consequences of their own godly or evil choices.

In addition to generational sin, Julie had the spirit of murder, for she testified she always wanted to die. The spirit of murder is a literal spirit without bodily form – a demon. This murdering spirit deceives the victim into death covenants. For example, speaking death over yourself such as, "I want to die," puts you in agreement with death. Understand that if the voice in your mind tells you to kill yourself because life is not worth living, that's not God. It is a demon speaking, and the more you mentally entertain suicide, the more you agree with that unclean spirit, giving it more ground to come into your life and torment you.

Then, once that unclean spirit is in, it will use many ways to murder you: drugs, self-harm, putting yourself in dangerous situations, entering threatening relationships, etc. It's all part of the devil's plan. Understand that each demon has a mission: the spirit of murder aims to kill, the spirit of addiction aims to hook you, etc. In Julie's case, we see the above spirits at play when she overdosed and stopped breathing.

Please understand that neither Satan nor his demons have power over us unless we give them power. And our power is given when we agree with their lies and mentally entertain their evil. God did not tell us to tolerate these demons nor to mentally entertain their evil. What we see in Julie's case is a spiritual war of the mind brought on by wrong teachings, flawed thinking, and disobedience to Christ; thus, she got tormented by suicidal thoughts. Instead, the Bible teaches us to pull down such demonic strongholds,

"Casting down arguments and every high thing that exalts itself against the knowledge of God, bringing every thought into captivity to the obedience of Christ" (2 Corinthians 10:4-5 NKJV).

God commands us to destroy demonic strongholds, overcome resistance, and break through barriers by using prayer and the Word of God as our spiritual weapons. These spiritual weapons access God's power to destroy the concentrated opposition of the enemy, particularly by demonstrating that the enemy's lies are false. Tools such as prayer and Scripture are powered by God, making them potent enough to destroy mental strongholds that resist the truth of Jesus. The battlefield in question is not an earthly region but the hearts and minds of the people held captive by Satan.

In God's power, the followers of Christ can destroy all the arguments and opinions the enemy puts forward against the knowledge of God. When a person has a proper understanding of God, they will have correct thinking, and obedience to Christ. In other words, the only way to capture evil thoughts and destroy is by obeying Christ. Without Christ, demonic attacks on our minds will continue. Due to these attacks on Julie's mind, she never experienced what it was like to want to live. She had no desire for life.

Jesus said, *"I am the resurrection and the life. He who believes in Me, though he may die, he shall live"* (John 11:25 NKJV).

Jesus is the life. If we do not know Jesus personally, we will not know life. No Jesus equals no life. Therefore, thinking we are safe just because we call ourselves Christians is silly. We are not safe until we know Christ personally. We must get intimate and profound in the presence of Christ.

Thankfully, Julie had a praying grandmother, who had praying friends in prison, whom the Holy Spirit led to pray for Julie on the day of her overdose. Let this be a lesson to us that we must never neglect the nudge of the Holy Spirit when we supernaturally wake up at three in the morning and can't sleep. Use this time to pray and intercede for those whom the Holy Spirit has put upon your heart, for you never know who is in danger during those early hours of the morning.

*"I exhort first of all that supplications, prayers, **intercessions**, and giving of thanks be made for all men" (1 Timothy 2:1 NKJV).*

After the prisoners prayed for Julie, she came back to life. Their intercession raised her from the dead. Just as Jesus and His disciples prayed and laid hands on the people, raising them from the dead, Julie testified that during the overdose, praying people surrounded her, laying hands on her before she came back to life. Reader, this is the grace of God.

So, how did locked up prisoners raise Julie from the dead who lay lifeless miles away? The answer is simple: Jesus can be anywhere at any time. He is not limited by time or space. Therefore, when a person intercedes for another person, God hears the prayer and is right there with the person in need. For instance, while Jesus was walking the earth in bodily form, He was in one place at a time. However, after ascending, by His Holy Spirit, He can be in multiple locations at once. He is omnipresent and omnipotent, existing everywhere, including inside and outside of time and space. It was not the prisoners who raise Julie from the dead, but the Holy Spirit working in and through the prisoners.

Jesus said to His believers, *"Most assuredly, I say to you, he who believes in Me, the works that I do he will do also; and greater works than these he will do, because I go to My Father" (John 14:12 NKJV).*

Raising the dead can be done from afar because it's not you going to the dead and raising them; it's Jesus by means of the Holy Spirit. Reader, this is one of the many greater works that Jesus told us we would do.

However, regardless of being raised from the dead, Julie still chose to continue in the addiction without seeking Jesus. Therefore, she sank lower. It was not until she decided to seek God for freedom from drugs that her life changed. Notice that Julie made a passionate plea to God, genuinely telling Him from her heart that she no longer wanted drugs. Julie was neither lukewarm in her petition, nor in two minds about quitting, nor doubting. She was serious that she wanted out. In other words, she surrendered all to God. Then God took addiction away, and she was free in an instant; not in twelve steps, but in an instant.

Please don't expect God to take away addiction when you still want to hold onto the habit. It would be best if you surrendered like Julie. I know a man in prison who was an addict for years. Sentenced to two years, he found more drugs in jail than on the streets. He continued drug use in prison, for he had no strength to quit. One day he turned to Jesus, prayed, and made a deal with Him, saying, "I will dedicate fifty-days of fasting and prayer to You if you give me the strength to quit the drugs." The man was set free in Jesus' Name on day fifty, with no cravings whatsoever. He is a free man. Notice that this prisoner and Julie had something in common: they surrendered to God.

After Julie invited God into her life and was set free, she made another passionate plea to Him to get the spirit of depression and suicide off her. God immediately answered, "Praise Me, because the devil doesn't like praise."

"The garment of praise for the spirit of heaviness" (Isaiah 61:3 NKJV).

In other words, the gladness and thanksgiving you feel when you get filled with praises and worship for the Lord are the opposite of a heavy heart. Praising God will lift you out of the heaviness, allowing you to push through into victory. When God told Julie to praise Him, He was teaching her spiritual warfare, for praise and worship are warfare tools. Then as she praised, the heaviness was lifted, defeating the devil in her life. God delivered her.

Suddenly God's voice became crystal clear, and the voice saying, "Kill yourself" was gone. God saved Julie's life. All spiritual chains that held her captive shattered, prison doors opened, and she was free.

"Oh, give thanks to the Lord, for He is good! For His mercy endures forever. Oh, give thanks to the God of gods! For His mercy endures

forever. Oh, give thanks to the Lord of lords! For His mercy endures forever: To Him who alone does great wonders, for His mercy endures forever; to Him who by wisdom made the heavens, for His mercy endures forever; to Him who laid out the earth above the waters, for His mercy endures forever; to Him who made great lights, for His mercy endures forever— the sun to rule by day, for His mercy endures forever; the moon and stars to rule by night, for His mercy endures forever" (Psalm 136:1-9 NKJV).

I FOUND HOPE AND PEACE IN JESUS

Marcus's Story
Growing up, I suffered from depression, anxiety, and low self-esteem. I had no hope of having a good life. My father drank alcohol heavily and chased us around the house to beat us. We had no money, and everything in the place was broken or damaged.

In 2020, I met Jesus for the first time. I called to Him, and He came and healed everything in my life. With Jesus, I experienced a peace that surpasses all understanding. I had never experienced so much peace before I met Him.

Before Christ, I read many books on depression, anxiety, and self-help, but I couldn't heal myself. But Jesus came and healed me instantly. With Jesus, I won the battle of smoking cigarettes, and all cravings vanished. Even my dad stopped drinking alcohol the same year I met Jesus. Jesus healed him too.

I have so much peace in my life with Jesus. My future is bright. I have hope and faith because I know that Jesus is the light in my future. He will never leave nor forsake me, and He loves me. I know that.

I used to wonder when the pain was going to stop. But now I have a happy life in Christ. Jesus' love transformed my life. Thank you, Jesus.
-Marcus

In Marcus's case, we see a broken house, a lack of money, and a destroyed home. We immediately know it's a spiritual attack on the family.

"The thief comes only to steal and kill and **destroy**" (John 10:10 NIV).

The powers of darkness oppressed Marcus's household. In addition, we see that he grew up with a dad who had a problem with alcohol addiction. In other words, dad battled with the spirit of addiction – this alone tells us that darkness operated in their household.

Please understand that when it comes to mind-altering substances like alcohol and drugs, it's an open doorway for demons to come into our lives. God did not tell us to get drunk. The Bible instructs:

"Do not get drunk on wine, which leads to debauchery. Instead, be filled with the Spirit" (Ephesians 5:18 NIV).

Reader, I warn you against being controlled by alcohol or drugs. Such substances lead to living a wasted and unproductive life. When we get drunk, we are not making the most of every opportunity; instead, we make unwise decisions. I am not saying that we must abstain from all alcohol; but we must not become intoxicated, for drunkenness can lead to all sorts of evil.

The Bible warns, *"Be sober, be vigilant; because your adversary the devil walks about like a roaring lion, seeking whom he may devour" (1 Peter 5:8 NKJV).*

Instead of alcoholic spirits, choose to be filled with the Holy Spirit. Just as drinking a great deal can cause a person to be controlled and steered by alcohol, focusing on the Holy Spirit can cause a person to be inspired and led by God's Spirit, thus living in a manner worthy of God's calling. Otherwise, alcohol and drugs will continue to sedate the mind, making the mind controlled by the devil, who eagerly awaits to hijack the reasoning of his victims. As the hijacked mind is an easy target, all sorts of evil can come in: distress, depression, and every other darkness Marcus experienced.

Prolonged depression opened doors to other problems like anxiety. We know Marcus was under the influence of darkness, for God does not tell us to be anxious. Instead, the Bible speaks against anxiety.

"Do not be anxious about anything, but in every situation, by prayer and petition, with thanksgiving, present your requests to God" (Philippians 4:6 NKJV).

Reader, can you see how ignorance of the Word of God and the inability to apply the Word can make your life move from bad to worse? Instead of anxiety, distress, or depression, we are to approach God humbly and gratefully with whatever is on our minds.

Sadly, most people do not know God; thus, they live in worry, anxiety, and hopelessness, as we see in Marcus's case, who testified, "I had no hope of a good life." This mental state of hopelessness is evident in many who have not come to God and do not know God. If they knew God, they would see He has a perfect plan for their lives; and that, regardless of their current situation, God can and will work through it to prosper them and give them a promising future.

*"For I know the thoughts that I think toward you, says the Lord, thoughts of peace and not of evil, to give you a future and a **hope**" (Jeremiah 29:11 NKJV).*

Marcus had a lousy upbringing, but he added additional suffering to his life by not knowing and trusting in God's promises of hope and a good future. It saddens me that people are ignorant of Jesus, the only One who can set man free from the darkness surrounding them. If only people knew that when Jesus comes into their lives the darkness would leave immediately.

"The light shines in the darkness, and the darkness has not overcome it" (John 1:5 NIV).

It baffles me why humankind rejects Christ, who is the light that will shine in their darkened soul. Fortunately, in 2020, Marcus met Jesus by calling to Him and thus was saved.

"Whoever calls on the name of the Lord shall be saved" (Romans 10:13 NKJV).

Jesus came and healed everything in Marcus's life. That's when Marcus experienced peace for the first time.

"Peace I leave with you, My peace I give to you; not as the world gives do I give to you. Let not your heart be troubled, neither let it be afraid" (John 14:27 NKJV).

Eternal peace is what Jesus promises. The peace that Jesus offers is unlike the superficial peace provided by the world that disappears in the face of adversity. The peace of Jesus is peace in the middle of the storm. Christ's peace is hope and reassurance beyond what a fallen world can offer. It is a permanent peace, guaranteed and eternal. I am not telling you to be stone-faced and inhuman, but to trust in God while in your suffering - this is the peace Marcus testified to experiencing.

When Jesus touched his life, peace and healing were instantaneous. Jesus broke the generational curse of addiction. Dad got delivered from alcohol, and Marcus got free from smoking cigarettes. Jesus freed the family.

"Believe on the Lord Jesus Christ, and you will be saved, you and your household" (Acts 16:31 NKJV).

Suddenly, Marcus's hopeless future turned bright, because Christ is the Light of the world who brings hope and faith to the darkened soul of man. Marcus now sees a bright life ahead, filled with hope that will never fade away.

"There is surely a future hope for you, and your hope will not be cut off" (Proverbs 23:18 NIV).

This Scripture is a promise for those whose hope is the Lord. Rest assured that God is faithful to His spoken Word, and what He says will come to pass, as it did for Marcus. Put your hope in Jesus, His faithfulness to keep His promises, and God's gift of grace and mercy to all who believe. Build your hope on nothing but Jesus Christ. Without Jesus, there is no hope. And if we foolishly put our hope in anything other than Christ and build our life upon that superficial foundation, we are destined to get disappointed. Therefore, wholly lean on Jesus, our solid Rock, just as Marcus did, because all other ground is sinking sand, temporary and short-lived.

Reader, the grace of God upon Marcus's life can happen for you also. But you must invite Christ into your heart and hope in Him. You either hope in people, places, and things, or you hope in Jesus. The choice is yours. I choose Christ.

"I will lift up my eyes to the hills— from whence comes my help? My help comes from the Lord, who made heaven and earth. He will not allow your foot to be moved; He who keeps you will not slumber. Behold, He who keeps Israel shall neither slumber nor sleep. The Lord is your keeper; the Lord is your shade at your right hand. The sun shall not strike you by day, nor the moon by night. The Lord shall preserve you from all evil; He shall preserve your soul. The Lord shall preserve your going out and your coming in from this time forth, and even forevermore" (Psalm 121: 1-8 NKJV).

TWENTY-YEAR-OLD HOMELESS CRACKHEAD

Jackson's Story
I went from a little boy who brought home straight A's to a boy who became a prodigal son. At 17, I became a crack cocaine addict for 20 years. I slept in broken, abandoned houses, underneath bridges, and in parking lots and sheds. I ate out of the trash and stole from grocery stores. I was completely ashamed of my hygiene and appearance. And that was my life for 20 years.

I moved from homeless shelter to homeless shelter. Then one day, after a failed suicide attempt, I woke up behind a dumpster and started crying. I located a Bible and began reading. Then I prayed, "God, why am I going through these challenges? Why can't I stop crack cocaine?" Then God led me to Ephesians 6:12:

"For we do not wrestle against flesh and blood, but against principalities, against powers, against the rulers of the darkness of this age, against spiritual hosts of wickedness in the heavenly places."

In Ephesians, God showed me that my battle for deliverance was against demon spirits that influenced me. Then God took me to Luke 4:1-13:

"Then Jesus, being filled with the Holy Spirit, returned from the Jordan and was led by the Spirit into the wilderness, being tempted for forty days by the devil. And in those days He ate nothing, and afterward, when they had ended, He was hungry. And the devil said to Him, 'If You are the Son of God, command this stone to become bread.' But Jesus answered him, saying, 'It is written, "Man shall not live by bread alone, but by every word of God."'
Then the devil, taking Him up on a high mountain, showed Him all the kingdoms of the world in a moment of time. And the devil said to Him, "All this authority I will give You, and their glory; for this has been delivered to me, and I give it to whomever I wish. Therefore, if You will worship before me, all will be Yours.'

And Jesus answered and said to him, 'Get behind Me, Satan! For it is written, "You shall worship the Lord your God, and Him only you shall serve."'
Then he brought Him to Jerusalem, set Him on the pinnacle of the temple, and said to Him, 'If You are the Son of God, throw Yourself down from here. For it is written: "He shall give His angels charge over you, to keep you," and, "In their hands they shall bear you up, lest you dash your foot against a stone."'
And Jesus answered and said to him, 'It has been said, "You shall not tempt the Lord your God."'
Now when the devil had ended every temptation, he departed from Him until an opportune time."

In Luke, God showed me that each time Jesus got tempted by the devil, He responded with, "It is written," followed by quoting the appropriate verse.

That day I decided to study the Bible to find all verses dealing with overcoming temptation. Then I used the Bible to overcome temptation. Now I am free. God set me free and changed my life.
-Jackson Miller

Reader, as we see in Jackson's case, the spirit of addiction influenced him. This unclean spirit took him through homelessness, eating out of the trash, and bad personal hygiene, to name a few. Jackson had no idea he was up against a demon spirit. Like most addicts, he probably thought his battle was against the substance.

Many addicts go to rehab to quit drugs. Others use medication to stop. Some even go through cold turkey. Each of these people thinks that the problem is the substance. Please understand that substance is not the issue here. The spirit of addiction is the issue. Addicts are up against a demon, not a drug. If they defeat the unclean spirit, the drug will have no power over them. But until the unclean spirit is defeated, it will influence them to chase the drug of choice.

Notice that it was not until Jackson started praying that God answered. Jackson asked God a legit question: "God, why is this happening to me?" Notice that Jackson did not blame, hate, or condemn God, as most people do. Instead, he asked God a valid question: "Why?" Then God spoke to Jackson through Scripture, revealing that his battle for deliverance from drugs was against demon spirits, not drugs. In other words, although Jackson was battling with physical drugs, the real problem was in the spiritual realm – an evil spirit.

Jackson needed to defeat the demon of addiction before he could be free, something only Christ could help him do. There is no other way to freedom but through Christ, for demons recognize and bow to the sovereignty of Jesus, no one else.

"All authority has been given to Me in heaven and on earth" (Matthew 28:18 NKJV).

Demons don't care if you are fed up with your life, if you want to stop drugs, or if you speak one hundred positive affirmations over your life. Unless you command the demon to leave with the authority of Jesus given to you, the demon will not leave. And that's why, when addicts attempt to quit drugs without Jesus, they end up moving from one addiction to the next:

- Heroin to alcohol addiction
- Cigarette to food
- Cocaine to sex
- Shopping to gambling addiction, etc.

In other words, you may quit heroin without Jesus, but you will quickly get hooked on alcohol as a substitute because the spirit of addiction is still there. You might stop cigarettes without Jesus, but you quickly crave food as a substitute because the demon of addiction is still there. Can you see how the problem is the unclean spirit who uses drugs, food, or gambling as bait to lure its victim into addiction? Addicts will continue to move from one obsession to the next because the problem is not the drugs, nor the substances, nor x, y, z. The problem is a demon. Unless Jesus steps in to cast out the demon, that demon will not leave. Invite Jesus into your heart; and with His might working in you, defeat the demon. Then you will no longer get and tempted by substances.

Again Jackson prayed, and God spoke through Scripture, leading him to a verse on defeating temptation. God led him to that specific verse because He wanted to show Jackson that, *"Each one is tempted when he is drawn away by his own desires and enticed"* (James 1:14 NKJV).

In other words, falling into temptation is due to the lusts, pleasures, and desires that already control us. These sinful desires exist within our hearts; thus, we are lured in by the sinful desires of our hearts. For example, a person weak to alcohol can get tempted by alcohol. A person vulnerable to seductive women can get seduced by such women. We cannot get tempted by something we do not like. The ungodly attitude already exists within the individual; for this reason, Satan can continue inducing the victim.

God did not tell Jackson to use drugs. God is against mind-altering substances. Though God tells you to stay away from the bait, when you are excited by the lure, Satan will tempt you with it; and, like a fish, you will get caught on the hook. In this manner, Satan uses your weaknesses as bait to lure you away. This bait will always promise to please or profit – but it's fake; and as you are allured and drawn by it, the temptation begins. Yet, throughout the enticement, God has His eye on you, testing you and waiting for you to acknowledge your wrongdoings and turn to Him so that He might give you strength and the way out.

When Satan tempted Jesus, Jesus did not fall for the lure, because there were no lusts, pleasures, or desires in Jesus that Satan could use to control Him.

Jesus said, *"He has nothing in Me"* (John 14:30 NKJV).

Be like Jesus. Jesus will help you and cleanse you of all sin and selfish appetites so that you no longer fall for the temptations of the evil one. Jesus will deliver you and give you strength to resist future temptations. Deliverance does not mean getting delivered from drugs. It means being free from the demon that influences you to do drugs.

And although many people claim that quitting drugs is not a quick process, I must disagree. If you look at the ministry of Jesus, you will notice that He healed the sick instantly. He cast out demons and raised the dead in an instant. For Jesus, it was a short process, a quick and easy action. With Jesus, deliverance is instantaneous. But beware: when Jesus delivers you, you must never return to slavery again.

"Stand fast therefore in the liberty by which Christ has made us free, and do not be entangled again with a yoke of bondage" (Galatians 5:1 NKJV).

With the Word of God, Jackson overcame temptation and got set free from the bondage of addiction. This is grace.

Notice what God did next. God continued to speak to Jackson through verses, forming a desire in him to look deeper into what God was saying, thus finding more verses that continued to deliver him. As in Jackson's case, Jesus is your key to freedom. Just as Jesus set Jackson free, He sets thousands free daily, and He can do the same for you, too.

"Then they cried out to the Lord in their trouble, and He saved them out of their distresses. He brought them out of darkness and the shadow of death, and broke their chains in pieces. Oh, that men would give thanks to the Lord for His goodness, and for His wonderful works to the children of men! For He has broken the gates of bronze, and cut the bars of iron in two" (Psalm 107:13-16 NKJV).

SHOT FIVE TIMES AND LEFT FOR DEAD

Jonathan's Story
At twenty-four years old, my life was all about becoming famous and making money. My friends had the same mentality. We traveled from location to location doing gigs and other performances. It was all about money, fame, and status. Yes, I knew of Christ, but had no interest in walking with Him.

One winter, I was travelling through the States with a group of friends. Arriving in one city, we found a hotel in a rough area of town. We checked in and took our luggage to our rooms. Everyone was tired and wanted to rest, but I was hungry, so I headed outside to a grocery store for food. It was the early hours of the morning. Standing on a street corner was a gang of nine or ten guys who started walking toward me. I continued walking as usual. The street was dark and empty.

The gang leader approached me first, and then all the gang members encircled me. The leader got up in my face, pulled out a gun, pointed it at me, and shot me. I fell to the ground. He stood over me, pointed the gun at me again, and fired another four shots.

I heard God speak to me, telling me to be still. So, I pretended to be dead until the gang left. Although I lay in a pool of my blood, I knew God was there right with me. I felt safe. When the gang finally ran off, I couldn't stand up. I couldn't feel anything. My body was numb from top to bottom. I tried to wave and signal cars to stop, but no one would stop. They just kept driving. They were probably scared. I reached for my phone and dialed 911.

It appeared that I would die, and all around me looked like life was coming to an end. Suddenly, I felt the urge to pray to Jesus. I began praying. Then the police and ambulance came. One paramedic said quietly to another, "He will not make it." I disregarded what I heard and continued to pray to Jesus. Upon reaching the hospital, I was immediately taken in for surgery. In the surgery room, I saw an angel standing in front of me. I did not doubt that everything was going to be ok. I felt immense peace, my breathing relaxed, and I fell asleep.

When I opened my eyes two days after surgery, I felt happy to be alive.
I know that I should have died, but by the grace of God, I am alive. The doctor walked in and confirmed that the surgery was a miracle from God. He stated that he alone could not have performed such a procedure. The doctor and I both agreed that God was the healer.

Today I am a minister for Christ. I travel and witness for Christ so that sinners come to salvation. My concern is no longer money, fame, and status but saving lost souls. Today I know that my experience was a means to bring many to Christ.
-Jonathan Jackson

Reader, in Jonathan's case, the problem started when his ambition for fame and money took over his life, leading him to a path that was not God ordained, but worldly. God did not tell him to chase money and fame, nor walk the streets alone late at night in a dangerous area of town. That was his choice to do so. Why do people walk through the valley of darkness and expect to be safe? This question baffles my mind.

"A prudent man foresees evil and hides himself, but the simple pass on and are punished" (Proverbs 22:3 NKJV).

In other words, the wise see danger ahead and avoid it, but the unwise keep going and get into trouble. Reader, I am confident God warned Jonathan to stop and change direction before disaster struck. The red flags were there all along; as Jonathan testified the gang started walking toward him, yet he failed to change direction to avoid them. God did not tell Jonathan to walk through the ghetto streets where death could be impending. To do so was Jonathan's choice. Shortly after, Jonathan was shot and left for dead.

Even after finding himself in a situation not ordained by God, God still spoke to him as he lay in his blood, telling him to *"Be still" (Psalm 46:10 NKJV)*.

Jonathan had a choice to obey or disobey God's direct command. Fortunately, he listened and remained motionless. Then God stepped in with a miracle: the gang took Jonathan for dead and never reshot him. Instead, they turned and walked away. Reader, can we see how God is always there to save us even in our worst life choices?

"I will deliver you from the hand of the wicked, and I will redeem you from the grip of the terrible" (Jeremiah 15:21 NKJV).

Although Jonathan lay in a pool of his blood, he felt safe, for he testified God's presence was there: "I know God was right there with me." Feeling safe and protected while lying in your blood with five bullet holes in your body is God's supernatural intervention. No one can give you such peace but Jesus.

"Peace I leave with you, My peace I give to you" (John 14:27 NKJV).

Suddenly Jonathan felt the nudge to pray to Jesus. Please understand that only the Holy Spirit can lead a person to pray to Christ.

"When He, the Spirit of truth, has come, He will guide you into all truth" (John 16:13 NKJV).

The Holy Spirit is the Spirit of truth who leads all people to the Truth. Christ is the Truth. How each person responds to the Spirit's lead is their choice; they can accept or reject the Truth. In Jonathan's case, he accepted the Spirit's call to prayer.

As the paramedics arrived, they ignorantly declared death over Jonathan: "He will not make it." Thankfully, Jonathan disregarded those spoken death spells and put his trust in God as he continued to pray, trusting the Lord to protect him.

"Though I walk through the valley of the shadow of death, I will fear no evil; for You are with me" (Psalm 23:4 NKJV).

Jonathan was in the valley of deep darkness; but by putting his complete trust in the protection of God, he got flooded with peace and hope. He lay in the ambulance fearlessly because he knew God was with him. It's interesting to observe that the shadow of death drew Johnathan closer to God.

Reader, God is with us when we walk over rough ground, just as He is with us beside still waters. Throughout the ambulance ride, God constantly reassured Jonathan that everything would be okay. Then God assigned His angel to stand by Jonathan's side as doctors prepared him for the operating room.

"For he will command his angels concerning you to guard you in all your ways" (Psalm 91:11 NIV).

Jonathan had no doubt, for He trusted God.

"If you can believe, all things are possible to him who believes" (Mark 9:23 NKJV).

When Jonathan opened his eyes after surgery, he was happy to be alive. No complaining or blaming God, just delight to be alive. He knew he was alive because of God's grace. Even the doctor testified the surgery was a miracle from God. That's a powerful testimony coming from a qualified professional.

Reader, is it not ironic that a near-death experience brought Jonathan closer to God? Today Jonathan is a minister of Christ, leading sinners to salvation. Hallelujah! Jonathan understands that his experience was a means to change direction in life, choose Christ, and bring many to the path of life.

Could God not have allowed other means less intense to draw Jonathan close to Him? Maybe He did use other means, but Jonathan didn't pay attention. Sometimes it takes a shock to get us to wake up and snap out of the worldly way of life.

"And the Lord shall help them and deliver them; He shall deliver them from the wicked, and save them, because they trust in Him" (Psalm 37:40 NKJV).

I MET JESUS IN THE MOUNTAINS

Tony's Story
I was a teen enjoying the summer with my friends in a small village in Italy. An evangelist approached us, handing out Jesus flyers. Although I didn't feel I needed it because I wasn't ill or depressed, I took it out of politeness because everyone else refused theirs. I placed the flyer in my wallet and forgot about it.

Hiking in the mountains one day, I sat for a rest. I sipped on water, then cleaned my wallet as I rested. The Jesus flyer fell out. I was ready to throw it away when the text caught my attention:

"Behold, I stand at the door and knock. And if any man hear my voice and open the door, I will come into him and fellowship with him, and he with me" (Revelation 3:20 NKJV).

Suddenly I felt a pull in my heart. That was Jesus knocking on the door of my heart. As I read the flyer text of Jesus knocking at the door of my heart, I simultaneously felt Him knocking on my heart to open for Him. I don't know how it happened, but I opened my heart's door and let Him in. And Jesus came flooding in.

I noticed that He is an actual living person. Jesus is alive. That day in the mountains, I met the living Christ. He moved through my soul like a wave. At that moment, all my sins got washed away. I could feel that the sins I had forgotten about were falling off me like old clothes. I felt clean. And I was made new.

"Behold, I make all things new" (Revelation 21:5 NKJV).

And He did make all things new in me on that day. While I was not looking for Jesus, He reached down and scooped me up. And in an instant, an undeserving person like me got saved.
-Tony Harrison

Reader, we see in Tony's case that he was not a bad kid who always got into trouble. He was an average kid who didn't know Jesus personally. Therefore, he did not know God's ways nor walk in His statutes.

God sent an evangelist to hand Tony a leaflet. Tony didn't feel he needed the Word of God but accepted the flyer to be friendly. Tony's attitude toward the flyer tells us he had no concept of his sins; therefore, he did not feel he needed a Saviour. But the Bible says differently:

"We are all like an unclean thing, and all our righteousnesses are like filthy rags; we all fade as a leaf, and our iniquities, like the wind, have taken us away" (Isaiah 64:6 NKJV).

Everyone has sinned. There is not one person that has not sinned.

"For all have sinned and fall short of the glory of God" (Romans 3:23 NKJV).

Thankfully, Tony took the leaflet, not because he felt he needed Jesus, but to be polite to the evangelist. That's when God spoke to him through the flyer: 'Jesus is knocking at the door of your heart."Reader, don't be cheated into believing that God doesn't speak to us through Scripture. He does. That's one of many ways God speaks to us.

"All Scripture is given by inspiration of God, and is profitable for doctrine, for reproof, for correction, for instruction in righteousness" (2 Timothy 3:16 NKJV).

As Tony read the written Word of God on the leaflet, God was speaking to him. Tony had a choice to accept or reject the call. He accepted. His heart opened to the idea of Jesus coming into His life. He was receptive; thus Jesus came in. Suddenly he experienced Jesus moving through his soul. Tony met the living Jesus in person. Immediately, he was aware of his sins, and he knew all his sins were wiped clean.

"In Him we have redemption through His blood, the forgiveness of sins, according to the riches of His grace" (Ephesians 1:7 NKJV).

Tony felt clean and cleansed. He testified he was made new.

"If anyone is in Christ, he is a new creation; old things have passed away; behold, all things have become new" (2 Corinthians 5:17 NKJV).

Jesus came knocking at Tony's heart as He comes knocking at all our hearts. Throughout our lives, Christ will consistently come to us, giving us opportunities to welcome Him into our lives. Whether through an evangelist, a YouTube video, a preacher, a church, Jesus in person, or any other means; Jesus comes continually to us. He has many ways of approaching us, knocking at the door of our hearts, as He did with Tony.

Reader, Jesus comes to you daily. Will you answer Christ's call, or will you reject Him? To those who hear the knock and open the door, Christ comes in.

"Behold, I stand at the door and knock. If anyone hears My voice and opens the door, I will come in to him and dine with him, and he with Me" (Revelation 3:20 NKJV).

Answer the call.

JESUS CAME TO ME IN SOLITARY CONFINEMENT

Peter's Story
I was an atheist all my life. In 2007 I went to prison for an assault. I got sentenced to four years. Things were going well for me in prison. I kept fit with physical exercise, the food was good, and I went out to work three days a week. It didn't feel like a prison.

But one day, I had a visit from my lawyer with news that I was charged with old criminal activity, facing a possible seven-year sentence. Four years plus another seven, I thought. That's eleven years. I froze. Suddenly my three kids came to mind who would grow up without me.

I got sent to a maximum-security prison. I was not adjusting well there. It all felt dark and violent. I got beaten up upon arrival. Bullet holes and blood scarred the prison walls. Suddenly deep depression hit me hard. I got lost in books of witchcraft and Buddhism to ease my pain. My cellmate was aggressive and abusive. I sat in my cell and cried about my life and family. I broke down. I was feeling suicidal. Immediately, I got taken to solitary confinement suicide watch.

I spent eighty days in solitary confinement on a 23-hour lockdown. At first, I enjoyed this time alone as I was away from violent inmates. I used this time to read more books on eastern religions. I learned to make Zen meditation and astral projection, which opened the door for demonic attacks. Very quickly, life became mentally and emotionally challenging. I began to feel trapped and alienated. I felt worse than ever. I was devastated and heartbroken. I felt hopeless, guilty, and abandoned.

"Pick up a Bible," said a voice in my mind, "Pick up a Bible." I got myself a Bible, opened it to Matthew, and started reading. I cried when I reached the chapter about Jesus's prayer in the Garden of Gethsemane: "Father, take this cup of suffering from Me."
This verse stuck in my mind and penetrated my being. Then in solitary confinement, I dropped to my knees and prayed to God. I

prayed the prayer that Jesus prayed in the garden: "God, take away from me this cup of suffering." I continued to pray, "I will dedicate my life to you. I will live the rest of my life serving others."

The next day, the mail arrived through the slot in my cell door. It was a letter from the public defender. I read the following words: "I have good news. The district attorney is thinking about dismissing the case. "I said, "Thank you, God."

God knew the lengths He had to go to recover me, and He took me there. It was on the brink of complete physical, moral, and spiritual poverty. It was where everyone turned their backs on me. In my despair, God came to me, knowing I would respond to Him due to desperation. He allowed the destruction of my life so he could give me a new one. He knew it would take a miracle before I believed, and He did just that.

Since then, He has worked miracle after miracle in my life, and the lives of family members. During the remaining time in prison, God's presence was prominent. The Holy Spirit developed in me an insatiable appetite to seek God, read the Bible, and fellowship with Him. Mental and emotional difficulties left me. Alienation, devastation, heartbreak, hopelessness, guilt, and feelings of abandonment were gone. It was all supernatural.

The day of my release from prison came, and I was free. Today I am a new person. Apart from rebuilding my life in Christ, I write Christian comics for children with imprisoned parents. God has chosen to use me in this way. I am grateful to Him.

I pray God uses me and my story even more so to touch the lives of many. I am devoted to prayer and faithful to the promise I made God in solitary confinement: "I want to serve God with all my heart." It is amazing what He has done for me and continues to do.
-Peter Maxwell

As we see with Peter, he had lived his whole life as an atheist. Atheism is a direct attack from Satan – it's a deception. Atheism is an open door for Satan to enter our lives and roam freely. The Bible warns:

"Do not give the devil a foothold" (Ephesians 4.27 NIV).

We must strive to keep Satan out of every aspect of our lives, because any open space we give the devil is too much space. Since Christ is our only strength to resist the devil, an atheist, who does not accept Christ, cannot possibly guard against enemy attacks. Therefore, atheism is an open doorway for the demonic. Atheists unknowingly rebel against God due to their lack of belief in God, which makes them an easy target for demonic deception: thinking they see while spiritually blind.

The Bible warns, *"Be sober, be vigilant; because your adversary the devil walks about like a roaring lion, seeking whom he may devour" (1 Peter 5:8 NKJV).*

We must constantly be on guard; this is something an atheist cannot do. Therefore, atheists are attacked continuously with all sorts of deceptions, as was Peter's case. Peter's life was filled with the devil's works: assault, violent prison inmates, feeling suicidal, etc. That's demonic stuff. That's not the Holy Spirit.

Then as demons tend to pave the way for the next unclean spirit to enter a person's life, before Peter knew it, deep depression hit him hard. Peter tried to escape these evil attacks by burying his head in occult books of Buddhism, not knowing that false religions and gods are first commandment violations.

"You shall have no other gods before Me" (Exodus 20:3 NKJV).

Ignorant of God's Word and warnings, Peter kept digging himself deeper into sin and darkness, slowly getting led to more occult books of witchcraft, which is another severe sin. God did not tell Peter to get involved in witchcraft. The Bible strictly warns against witchcraft. *"He practiced soothsaying, used witchcraft and sorcery, and consulted mediums and spiritists. He did much evil in the sight of the Lord" (2 Chronicles 33:6 NKJV).*

The seeking of supernatural powers other than God is evil in God's eyes. It's demonic. Satan has used witchcraft to prevent people from finding holy spirituality in God. He uses occult practices such as mediums, horoscopes, and new age spirituality, to entice people away from God toward a power that gives a false sense of self-enlightenment. Please understand that there are demonic consequences of following such falsehood. These demonic attacks that followed Peter in the form of suicidal thoughts were spirit demons attacking his mind, emotions, and body.

Peter testified to feeling alienated. Alienation is a feeling of estrangement when we separate ourselves from the One who created us – God. Yet even in Peter's rebellion against God, God still spoke to him, saying, "Pick up a Bible." Reader, this is the love and grace of God toward sinners, for He is *"patient with you, not wanting anyone to perish, but everyone to come to repentance" (2 Peter 3:9 NIV).*

Fortunately, Peter obeyed God's voice and picked up a Bible. Then God spoke to him through Scripture. As God spoke, something shifted in Peter, because, in his hopeless despair as an atheist, he dropped down on his knees and prayed to God: "God, take this suffering from me, and I will dedicate my life to you." Wow! Reader, what a fantastic transformation: from being an atheist to praying and asking for God's help.

God answered Peter's prayer and touched his life, changing, healing, and delivering him – this is grace. Notice that it was not until Peter opened his heart to God that God's presence became prominent in Peter's prison cell. Understand that God's presence was always with Peter, but Peter needed to let go of skepticism and open his heart to God before he could perceive God's presence. Let this be a lesson to us all: God's presence is with us wherever we go, but, although He is there, we do not perceive Him when our hearts are of stone. Sadly, this is a mistake atheists make. They harden their hearts toward God and then proclaim God does not exist because they cannot perceive Him.

Notice that once Peter's heart was open, the Holy Spirit developed within him a strong appetite for God, a desire to read the Bible, and a hunger for fellowship with God. Through the Holy Spirit, Peter rebuilt his life and now does Kingdom work to help touch the lives of others who are suffering as he suffered – this is grace.

Reader, it is essential to note that the suffering Peter experienced resulted from his bad choices. God permits us to suffer the consequences of our sinful choices so that we learn from our mistakes, grow, and spiritually mature. However, if we continue to rebel against God and refuse to learn, the suffering is prolonged – again, this is our choice. God knows the lengths we must go through to recover us, and He will let us go there if we insist.

In Peter's case, he needed to go to the brink of complete physical, moral, and spiritual poverty. God allowed the destruction of Peter's life so He could give Peter a new life in Christ, free of evil and destruction. Many people require a miracle before they believe in God. In such cases, God may allow them to reach rock bottom, so He can work His miracle in the impossible, thus bringing them to a place of belief in God.

Reader, it's incredible what God has done in the life of a suicidal atheist, sentenced to prison, and bound to witchcraft – this is the grace of God. If God did it for Peter, He can do it for you, too. Thus, if you are in a similar situation as Peter, remember:

"In my distress I cried to the Lord, and He heard me" (Psalm 120:1 NKJV).

I FOUND LOVE AFTER STEPFATHER'S SEXUAL ABUSE

Tina's Story
Before coming to Christ, I had heard of Him but didn't know Him. My household was anything but holy. My childhood was difficult and rough. My stepfather begun to sexually abuse me at age four, and this continued for seven years. The abuse stopped at age eleven when I was at the age to report him.

My whole upbringing was harrowing and filled with brokenness. After many years of keeping the abuse secret, I finally spoke up. I told my closest cousin, and she told her counselor. My mum heard what my stepdad did to me, but, hypnotized by her love for this man, she didn't understand. I always protected her when he beat her black and blue, which made me sadder that she didn't believe me. She called me a liar and blamed me; then, she rejected me.

While the police were investigating the abuse case, my mum sent me to foster care rather than have my abuser leave. I felt broken, abandoned, and lost. That's when I rebelled and became a runaway.

Growing up, I lacked a father's love. Due to getting hurt by the only father figure I knew, I unintentionally began to hurt men. How could I love someone when I didn't know what love looked like? Haunted by my past, I entered a marriage that failed instantly. Divorce followed. I started drinking large amounts of alcohol to forget and numb the pain. I kept hurting others and myself. It wasn't intentional; I couldn't stop myself.

I wanted the pain to end; I wanted to feel loved and show love to others truly. That's when I decided to turn to the only One who I could trust. I devoted my life to Jesus Christ, my Saviour. He taught me to love. I felt His love deep within my heart. He taught me how to talk with Him and love Him back.

It was unconditional love. A love I have never known before. It was real love.

I am a new mum who shows the love of Christ to my children. I will never allow my children to live a day without knowing the love of Christ. Jesus changed my life and my children's lives. I feel at peace. My life was darkened by my past hurts, and Jesus shone His light. His light now guides me.

Please welcome Jesus into your life as I did. You will experience His unconditional love. Accepting Jesus was the best decision I made.
-Tina Watson

As we see in Tina's case, she had heard of Jesus from a young age but never knew Him personally. She had no relationship with Him. Jesus was not a part of her life. Unfortunately, we see this with many Christians today, only knowing Christ with their lips, not their hearts.

"These people draw near to Me with their mouth, and honor Me with their lips, but their heart is far from Me" (Matthew 15:8 NKJV).

It's sad how many parents bring up their children not knowing Christ. It's also unfortunate that many parents make their household an open door for enemy intrusion. As in the case of Tina, who was sexually abused by her stepdad, once the intruder is given entry, a child endures much suffering and darkness in their upbringing.

The parent is the head of the household, so if the head stinks, the whole body will follow in that same stench. The parent is supposed to be the child's protector, but if the protector becomes the child's harmer, the child's open wounds will make them vulnerable to the demonic. As an example of this, we see Tina's mum choosing her abusive lover over Tina, thus rejecting her child. If taken to heart, this abandonment can open doors for the spirit of rejection to enter the child's life, as was in Tina's case.

With the spirit of rejection operating in Tina's life, she began to exhibit those exact attributes; thus, she started to reject and hurt men herself. Thus, Tina begun to manifest more darkness in her life and surroundings. That's how easily people become vessels for darkness, bringing more hurt, pain, and suffering into the world.

Tina testified: "It wasn't intentional, for I couldn't stop myself." When a person can't stop themselves, it implies no self-control. Understand that self-control is a fruit of the Holy Spirit; therefore, lack of self-control is not of God, but of the evil one, who wants to control you so that he can destroy you. Children of God live in self-control, but those not of God, who are of the world are *"under the control of the evil one" (1 John 5:19 NIV).*

Understand that compulsive behaviors imply that something controls you. Where you see control and manipulation, there is usually witchcraft involved. And if all that weren't enough, Tina's marriage also failed.

Sadly, all these open wounds invite demons to come and feed off Tina's injuries. For example, Beelzebub gets mentioned in the Bible as the ruler of the demons (Mark 3:22). Beelzebub gets translated as 'lord of flies.' As flies like to land on open skin wounds to feed, in the same manner, demons like to feed off people's mental and emotional injuries, hurts, and pains. In other words, Tina's wounds were an open door for demons to feast.

Her brokenness opened the door for all sorts of unclean spirits to enter her life. That's how easily evil enters and takes over a child's life, destroying their childhood and adulthood. By adulthood, Tina's life was crawling with demonic influence, paving the way for the spirit of addiction to sneak in. Then with alcohol in the picture, her mind became more susceptible, where demons could influence to a deeper level, causing the victim to say and do all sorts that she would not usually do, such as hurting self and others, manifesting more darkness, etc.

The Bible warns, saying, *"Be alert and of sober mind. Your enemy the devil prowls around like a roaring lion looking for someone to devour"* (1 Peter 5:8 NIV).

Tina's life kept going from bad to worse. It was not Tina's fault that abuse, and other nasty things happened to her as a child. However, growing up and reaching an age of reason, she had free will to turn to God rather than inflict her pain on others; thus, doing to other people what got done to her. God did not tell Tina to impose that darkness on others. That was her sinful choice.

The Bible states, *"And just as you want men to do to you, you also do to them likewise"* (Luke 6:31 NKJV).

When Tina had grown up, and was able to make her own choices, she chose the voice of Satan over the voice of God, giving more ground for the enemy to stand, thus prolonging her suffering.

It wasn't until she decided to turn to Christ that everything started to shift for the better. Tina dedicated her life to Christ, and Jesus taught her a genuine love that she never received as a child. With the revelation of Jesus' love, Tina could genuinely love others back, for now she knew true love, unconditional and absolute.

"Love is from God, and whoever loves has been born of God and knows God" (1 John 4:7 NKJV).

It was then that Tina could release that love to her children. She was no longer a vessel for Satan, manifesting darkness, but now she was a vessel for Christ, manifesting His love to her family.

Due to Christ's love, Tina could love her kids, breaking the generational curse of abuse and rejection that got passed down to her. Jesus came into Tina's life, and all unclean spirits had to leave, because the authority of Christ was getting executed.

"In Him was life, and the life was the light of men. And the light shines in the darkness, and the darkness did not comprehend it" (John 1:4-5 NKJV).

Today Jesus is the light in Tina's life, guiding and protecting her from the schemes of the evil one. The key to such major transformation is Jesus. Notice that Tina's life changed only when she chose the path of Christ. Reader, we all have free will to choose whether we will come to Christ or allow Beelzebub to continue feeding off our childhood wounds. The choice is ours because God gave us free will. If you are a youth experiencing a similar misfortune as Tina, you can turn to Christ and allow Him to help and guide you. Also, pray that your parents get delivered from the darkness that envelopes them and that their hearts be opened to receive Christ. God bless you.

I CAN DO ALL THROUGH CHRIST

Alicia's Story
From the age of five years old to the age of eight, I was abused and raped. I got left with scars and brokenness. I hated men because they hurt me badly. Growing up, I figured that a girl would be the only person who couldn't hurt me anymore. So I became a lesbian. She, also, was abusive, and I ended up hating her, too.

My mom forced me to go to church. Although I didn't want to, I had no other choice. It was there that God worked in my life. I got saved. Jesus was the only One who could take the bad out of my life and make a masterpiece. He changed my life.

He put my life back in order. He removed me from my abusive lesbian relationship, mended my broken family, and healed my old hurts. He gave me reasons to want to live. He has been good to me. He gave me a new home, a new life, and a new church with new friends. God gave me all I needed with His Son, Jesus Christ. I'm getting stronger because God is working in my life. Thank you, Lord.
-Alicia

Reader, Alicia is another case where a child gets mistreated and molested by adults. In God's eyes, children are a reward from God.

"Children are a heritage from the Lord, the fruit of the womb is a reward" (Psalm 127:3 NKJV).

Children are a gift to be cherished, not mistreated. We see a lot of abuse against children from adults who are not operating under the authority of God.

By authority, I mean that, *"The head of every man is Christ, the head of woman is man, and the head of Christ is God" (1 Corinthians 11:3 NKJV).*

Every person has a head—man, woman, or Christ Himself. Each of us is under the authority of someone. The head of Christ is God, the head of man is Christ, the head of a wife is her husband, and the head of children is the parent. And all answer to God - this is the design and order of creation.

If a man, who is the head of the house, is not representing Christ, who is his head, then the wife and children have no business following him into sin and destruction. Many children suffer because the head of the house is not operating under the authority of God.

Sadly, in addition to the parents, often the church of Christ does not represent Christ well. In other words, the world continues in wickedness, not because of corrupt politicians, but because most of the church of Christ is not doing its job of sharing the gospel, making disciples, healing the sick, casting out demons, teaching people to walk as Jesus instructed, and manifesting heaven on earth. The church sleeps while people perish in a dying world. If the church sleeps, there is no one to educate the adults, no one to war against spiritual forces of evil, no one to keep Alicia covered by the blood of Christ, and no one to pray for the children.

If the blood of Christ covered Alicia, no abuser could touch that child. But as the church and parents sleep, spiritual forces of evil are destroying families. Once these evil influences are operating in a person's life, it's common to see abominations such as women turning to lesbianism for love and acceptance, as was Alicia's case.

It's good that Alicia's mum forced her to go to church, where she found God, got saved, and the Holy Spirit started working a masterpiece in her life. Praise our Lord, Jesus Christ, for healing, delivering, and changing her life completely, putting all brokenness back into divine order. Jesus removed from her every darkness: abuse, lesbianism, hate, hurt, distrust, etc. Alicia's wounds were healed, and the abomination of lesbianism was broken. Jesus gave her a reason to want to live again. He gave her hope.

"Our Savior and the Lord Jesus Christ, our hope" (1 Timothy 1 NKJV).

Jesus not only came to bring hope; He is our hope. We have hope because Jesus forgives us and transforms us into his likeness. Hallelujah! Alicia testified: "All in my life is new: home, life, church, friends." Reader, this is a promise of Jesus to all who turn to Him: *"Behold, I make all things new" (Revelation 21:5 NKJV).*

If Christ can turn Alicia's life around, He can do it for you, too.

"Do not fret because of evildoers, nor be envious of the workers of iniquity. For they shall soon be cut down like the grass, and wither as the green herb. Trust in the Lord, and do good; dwell in the land, and feed on His faithfulness. Delight yourself also in the Lord, and He shall give you the desires of your heart. Commit your way to the Lord, trust also in Him, and He shall bring it to pass. He shall bring forth your righteousness as the light, and your justice as the noonday. Rest in the Lord, and wait patiently for Him; do not fret because of him who prospers in his way, because of the man who brings wicked schemes to pass. Cease from anger, and forsake wrath; do not fret—it only causes harm. For evildoers shall be cut off; but those who wait on the Lord, they shall inherit the earth. For yet a little while and the wicked shall be no more; indeed, you will look carefully for his place, but it shall be no more. But the meek shall inherit the earth, and shall delight themselves in the abundance of peace" (Psalm 37:1-11 NKJV).

HINDU LEADER TO JESUS CHRIST

Sri's Story
I am a Hindu RSS leader (Rashtriya Swayamsevak Sangh) with a respectable position in India. In 1995 I attended a Christian meeting and heard the message of Jesus as Saviour. After hearing the message of Christ, my heart started pounding. I felt supernatural power working in me.

After the meeting, I approached the pastor and asked him about a verse I heard him preach: "I am the way, the truth, and the life. No one comes to the Father except through Me" – John 14:6.

This verse stuck in my mind. I was eager to know its meaning. After explaining the verse, the pastor prophesied over me that soon I would be a minister for Christ. A still voice kept repeating: "I am the way, the truth, and the life. No one comes to the Father except through Me."

I returned home and prayed into thin air, saying, "Whoever is speaking to me, if You are the real God, please appear to me." Then, a bright white light came, and I fell to the floor. I woke up after twenty minutes or so. That's when I received a revelation that I had seen Jesus.

Then out of the blue, someone came and handed me a Bible. I didn't know what it was then, but they told me to study the book. That night as I was sleeping, a voice woke me. I opened my eyes and saw no one but a bright light shining upon the Bible. I opened the book and started reading. That's when I realized that Jesus is the real God.

I removed all religious items and threw them in the bin. I began telling people that Jesus is the real God. Friends and family rejected me, but I didn't care because I knew Jesus in person. Since then, I got baptized in the Name of the Father, the Son, and the Holy Spirit.

I attended over 200 churches and gave my testimony. I told them about the gift of salvation found in Jesus, the power of the blood of

Jesus that cleans all our old sins, and that Jesus will change them and make them holy so that they can stand before our Father in heaven. Many people have believed the message of Christ and converted.
-Sri

Reader, in Sri's case, we see a severe sin: worshipping false gods. To do so is a first commandment violation:

"You shall have no other gods before Me" (Exodus 20:3 NKJV).

The spirit of religion that operated in Sri's life is a demonic spirit that influences a person, or group of people, to replace a genuine relationship with the One true living God with works and traditions; thus, preventing people from going before the true living God. The religious spirit is very deceptive. It will influence you into putting fake gods and religions before God so that you are not in a relationship with God. Do not be deceived into religions and false gods. It's a trap of the evil one.

Instead, ask God to reveal Himself to you. Ask Him to help you focus on Him so that you continually turn your mind and heart towards Him. Learn to love Him supremely. Everything in your life must flow from your personal relationship with God. Otherwise, the devil will deceive you through false gods and religions, causing you to think that you can see clearly while being spiritually blind.

Religion is very deceptive. "*They are blind leaders of the blind. And if the blind leads the blind, both will fall into a ditch*" *(Matthew 15:14 NKJV).*

Fortunately, Sri attended a Christian meeting where he heard the message of Christ, which proceeded to him calling out to God.

"Whoever calls on the name of the Lord shall be saved. How then shall they call on Him in whom they have not believed? And how shall they believe in Him of whom they have not heard? And how shall they hear without a preacher? And how shall they preach unless

they are sent? As it is written: 'How beautiful are the feet of those who preach the gospel of peace, who bring glad tidings of good things!' But they have not all obeyed the gospel. For Isaiah says, 'Lord, who has believed our report?' So then faith comes by hearing, and hearing by the word of God" (Romans 10:13-17 NKJV).

God promises that those who call to Christ in faith will be saved. But how can anyone call on Christ if they don't believe in Him? Therefore, before calling on Christ, one must believe in Him. But how can anyone believe in Christ if they have never heard of Him? Therefore, before believing in Christ, one must hear of Him. But how will anyone hear about Christ if no one preaches Christ to them? Therefore, before one can hears about Christ there must by those who preach Christ.

For this reason, preaching Christ is necessary. If Sri had not heard of Christ, he could not have believed in Christ; thus, he would not have called on Christ to get saved by Christ. Let this be a message to all followers of Christ: "We must preach the message of Christ."

Sri testified that after hearing the message of Christ, his heart started pounding. That was Christ knocking at the door of his heart.

"Behold, I stand at the door and knock. If anyone hears My voice and opens the door, I will come in to him and dine with him, and he with Me" (Revelation 3:20 NKJV).

The still voice repeating, "I am the way, the truth, and the life. No one comes to the Father except through Me," was God calling to Him. Sri could have chosen to deny the still voice, as many people do, but he didn't. Instead, he returned home and decided to pray, saying: "Whoever You are, if you are the real God, appear to me." Suddenly, a bright light appeared to him. The Bible tells us who the light is:

Then Jesus spoke to them again, saying, *"I am the light of the world. He who follows Me shall not walk in darkness, but have the light of life" (John 8:12 NKJV).*

Jesus is the light that appeared to Sri. But beware, the Bible warns of false light: *"Satan himself masquerades as an angel of light" (2 Corinthians 11:4 NIV).*

Reader, take heed that you do not mistake Satan's counterfeit light for the light of Christ, thinking you are living righteous when you are not. The light of Christ will always lead you to the Father in heaven. It will never conflict with the living Word of God. It will change you from the inside out, leading you into all truth. You will have peace that surpasses all understanding. When Jesus touches you, you will never be the same again.

With Satan's counterfeit, you will get lost in doctrines and false gods and religions. Confusion will hit you, peace will be lacking, and inner transformation will not follow. You will remain the same, living in sin, claiming righteousness while being a hypocrite. That's not the light of Christ.

I have witnessed that when we let go of all religious views, doctrines, ideas, and all spiritual teachings, and we genuinely ask for truth while humbly acknowledging that we don't know the truth, the real God will appear, and we will find that He is the Jesus of the Holy Bible.

For example, Sri humbly let go of all old religious beliefs and doctrines of false gods and asked for the real God to step forth. That's when Jesus came to him as a light. Sri accepted Jesus as his Lord and thus his eyes opened to the truth. He was convicted to throw out all religious items, and he was set free from the spirit of religion. That's called deliverance – that's what I mean being transformed by the real light.

Sri's whole life changed. He got baptized and began preaching Jesus, becoming a part of the Great Commission:

Jesus said, *"Go therefore and make disciples of all the nations, baptizing them in the name of the Father and of the Son and of the*

Holy Spirit, teaching them to observe all things that I have commanded you; and lo, I am with you always, even to the end of the age" (Matthew 28:18-20 NKJV).

The Great Commission is the instruction of the resurrected Jesus Christ to His disciples to spread the gospel to all the world's nations, sharing God's love in word and deed. As Christians, we are to spread the Word of God to the nations, demonstrate God's love, and pray for God to raise up missionaries.

Persecution will come against us for doing so, but we must remain faithful, as Sri did. Sri received persecution from family and friends, but he stayed loyal to Jesus, and we are to do the same.

"Blessed are you when they revile and persecute you, and say all kinds of evil against you falsely for My sake. Rejoice and be exceedingly glad, for great is your reward in heaven, for so they persecuted the prophets who were before you" (Matthew 5:11-12 NKJV).

We are blessed when we endure persecution for the sake of righteousness. Blessed are we when we willingly endure unfair treatment for faithfully following Christ. Those in opposition to Jesus might insult us, abuse us, and falsely accuse us of doing terrible things. But regardless of trails, we must remain faithful, as Sri did.

Today Sri is saved by placing his faith and trust in the finished work of Christ on the cross. He travels and preaches Christ, converting many through his testimony. Hallelujah, praise the Lord! This is grace.

"Your mercy, O Lord, is in the heavens; Your faithfulness reaches to the clouds. Your righteousness is like the great mountains; Your judgments are a great deep; O Lord, You preserve man and beast. How precious is Your lovingkindness, O God! Therefore the children of men put their trust under the shadow of Your wings. They are abundantly satisfied with the fullness of Your house, and You give

them drink from the river of Your pleasures. For with You is the fountain of life; in Your light we see light" (Psalm 36:5-9 NKJV).

I SAW THE LIGHT OF CHRIST

Jimmy's Story
I want to tell you about the darkness I made for myself as I followed the crowds and did everything they did. Like a spreading disease, the devil marches with his followers: seductive women, alcohol abusers, drug users, money lovers, etc. Like many teens, I hung out with the devil and his followers. I did the sex, drugs, and party scene. I was only 16, and playing in the devil's territory brought darkness into my life. I pretended to be happy and not to care, but it was a lie. I was desperate, depressed, and lost. I didn't want to tell my parents how miserable I was, so I suffered alone. I felt my life deteriorating by the day. Drugs and alcohol were daily, and sexual one-night stands became normal. Although I continued to drink from the devil's cup, God had some strong saints praying for me: my mother, grandmother, and auntie.

One day God said to me: "All things are possible through Christ." If that is true, I thought to myself, then I don't need alcohol anymore; nor do I need seductive women and drugs. "God, if what you say is true, then free me from my darkness," I prayed. I was instantly set free. It was an immediate transformation. Yes, I did my part of resisting sin, but God was faithful to His word of promise in that if I would resist sin, then He would cover and protect me.

Today I stand in the light of Jesus Christ. There is no more darkness in my life. Jesus is my light, and I live for Him.
-Jimmy Stronghold

Jimmy testifies that darkness came upon him due to living a worldly life, following sinful people into destruction. God did not tell Jimmy to live such a life. That was his choice. Jimmy's choices led him to walk in darkness, where Christ's light was not experienced. Understand that where we see darkness, there is sin; where there is sin, there is darkness. The two are linked.

Jimmy got lost in a sinful worldly life of seductive women, drugs, alcohol abuse, and money-loving, because he let himself get tempted by these things. Jimmy's lifestyle was not God's plan for his life. We know this because the Bible warns against worldliness:

"Do not be conformed to this world, but be transformed by the renewing of your mind, that you may prove what is that good and acceptable and perfect will of God" (Romans 12:2 NKJV).

To live a worldly life is to conform to the world and its patterns so that we become shaped into its ways. When people conform to the world, they are taking on its likeness. We are not to follow the worldly way of life but rather get transformed by a renewed mind. A renewed mind is an inner reality of God's presence. In other words, this transformation happens when we surrender to God. There is no other way.

"Present your bodies a living sacrifice, holy, acceptable to God, which is your reasonable service" (Romans 12:1 NKJV).

This inner transformation eventually makes its way to the surface of your life for everyone to see. But the outward change that people notice begins with an inward change which only God sees. Without this transformation, you will continue in darkness, as Jimmy did for many years. Such a life of following the crowds and doing everything they do is a spreading disease that puts us deeper into the ways of the evil one. Take my advice:

"Do not give the devil a foothold" (Ephesians 4:27 NIV).

Give Satan no openings into your life by living a worldly life of sin. Instead, stand against his evil schemes. Diligently work to keep the devil from having an opportunity or advantage by guarding against any area of life that might compromise your walk with the Holy Spirit. Suppose you fail to keep the devil out of your life. In that case, the demonic will enter and hold you in bondage, and you will experience what Jimmy underwent: depression, feeling lost, desperation, misery, and suffering, to name a few. Jimmy's sinful lifestyle led him to a tormented life, and his deterioration began.

"For the wages of sin is death" (Romans 6:23 NKJV).

Although Jimmy didn't want that sinful life, he didn't understand how to exit, for he didn't know Christ. Fortunately, he had family members covering him in prayer. They stood in the gap for him through intercession, and God heard their supplication, for, *"The prayer of a righteous person is powerful and effective" (James 5:16 NIV).*

Then one day, God answered their plea and spoke to Jimmy: "All things are possible in Christ." Jimmy had the option to respond or ignore God's spoken words, as do we all. Fortunately, he responded by replying, "God, if what You say is true, save me from the darkness." God immediately freed Jimmy from the darkness surrounding him. Reader, notice that Jimmy worked together with God. Jimmy did not do all the work, neither did God control him robotically. It was teamwork, a beautiful collaboration between a loving Father and His child. Jimmy did his part by turning to God and resisting the devil's temptation of seductive women, drugs, alcohol, etc. What Jimmy did is biblical:

"Submit to God. Resist the devil and he will flee from you" (James 4:7 NKJV).

Only from the place of God's presence Jimmy had the strength to resist the temptations of the evil one; thus, the devil fled. Jimmy testified that he is now free from darkness and walks in Christ's light.

"I am the light of the world. He who follows Me shall not walk in darkness, but have the light of life" (John 8:12 NKJV).

Reader, God's living Word is true, alive, and active. When we apply the living Word, the Word will manifest in and around us, changing us from the inside out and transforming our surroundings.

I speak from experience when I say, "You don't need to put up with darkness a day longer. Jesus came to set you free from that. Call upon His Name and be saved today."

"Praise the Lord! I will praise the Lord with my whole heart, in the assembly of the upright and in the congregation. The works of the Lord are great, studied by all who have pleasure in them. His work is honorable and glorious, and His righteousness endures forever. He has made His wonderful works to be remembered; the Lord is gracious and full of compassion. He has given food to those who fear Him; He will ever be mindful of His covenant. He has declared to His people the power of His works, in giving them the heritage of the nations. The works of His hands are verity and justice; all His precepts are sure. They stand fast forever and ever, and are done in truth and uprightness. He has sent redemption to His people; He has commanded His covenant forever: Holy and awesome is His name" (Psalm 111:1-9 NKJV).

HEALED FROM HIV

Stephanie's Story
After having unprotected sex, I was diagnosed with the symptom of HIV. I started suffering from stress, depression, anxiety, and insomnia. I had constant diarrhea, night sweat, fever, fatigue, dry cough, and extreme weight loss. HIV was attacking my immune system. My whole life caved in around me.

I searched the net for the healing miracle of HIV but found nothing. Then I started praying continuously to God to heal me, "God, heal me, God, heal me," I prayed repeatedly. As I prayed, I had faith God would heal me. I continued to pray daily. God heard my prayers, and He did a miracle. He healed me. All my sickness disappeared, and I was healed through the power of God, who strengthened me. I am HIV-free. Now I live a normal life with my loved ones. God is the true and only God. Praise God.
-Stephanie Dixon

Reader, let's look at the spiritual side of Stephanie's story. There was sin in Stephanie's life through fornication. Know there will be dark consequences when sin is executed, for sin and darkness intertwine. Sin opens the door to demonic influence, bringing darkness into an individual's life. Most people blame God for their problems when most of their problems come from not listening to God. For instance, the Bible is clear that God is not happy with fornicators.

*"Do not be deceived. Neither **fornicators**, nor idolaters, nor adulterers, nor homosexuals, nor sodomites, nor thieves, nor covetous, nor drunkards, nor revilers, nor extortioners will inherit the kingdom of God" (1 Corinthians 6:9-10 NKJV).*

All sexual immorality is a sin. Sexual immorality is every kind of sex outside of heterosexual marriage: adultery, homosexual acts, fornication, prostitution, rape, sex with children, sex with animals, etc. Such people will not inherit God's kingdom, for all forms of sexual immorality are deeply and unmistakably sinful. Understand that how one chooses to live life and how one chooses to use their body reflects their relationship with Christ. Embracing sinful behaviors shows a profound rejection of God. That's why God commands us to flee from sexual immorality.

"Flee from sexual immorality. Every other sin a person commits is outside the body, but the sexually immoral person sins against his own body. Or do you not know that your body is a temple of the Holy Spirit within you, whom you have from God? You are not your own, for you were bought with a price. So glorify God in your body" (1 Corinthians 6:18-20 NKJV).

God designed our bodies to serve Him. We are to use our bodies to bring glory to Him. When we follow God's ways, we are protected under the shadow of the Almighty. But when we rebel, we give ground to the devil, making ourselves susceptible to dark consequences such as HIV, and more alike. That's not the plan God has for us. God wants us to live in the light, in freedom, and in good health. It is our choice to sin that brings detrimental consequences, for sin brings a curse. In other words, where there is sin, there is a curse, and where there is a curse, there is sin. Our choice to live sinfully is our consent that invites demonic torment. Seriously, we can't expect to sin and be blessed at the same time.

In addition to the sin of fornication, Stephanie had unprotected sex. The devil wants nothing more than to give all fornicators sexually transmitted disease (STD), as in Stephanie's case, who contracted HIV. Again, such dark consequences stem from sin and rebellion against God. God doesn't want us walking around with HIV - that's the devil's plan. God wants us to walk as Christ walked: in freedom, power, and authority.

Stephanie's life was losing its value daily as she suffered from persistent HIV symptoms. As Stephanie's life came crumbling down, she made another mistake by searching for healing methods online rather than turning to her Creator for healing.

"Asa became diseased in his feet, and his malady was severe; yet in his disease he did not seek the Lord, but the physicians. So Asa rested with his fathers; he died in the forty-first year of his reign" (2 Chronicles 16:12-13 NKJV).

Trusting human strength and leaving God out of the picture is not good. It is sad that Stephanie stopped trusting the Lord and began searching the net for alternative healing instead. Such is the deceptive mentality of many worldwide, where people put physicians above God. Please do not misinterpret what I am saying: Seeking physicians for help with a disease does not necessarily mean a reproach from God so long as you also seek the Lord. Yes, give honor to a physician when recognition is due, but healing comes from the Lord.

"Bless the Lord, O my soul, and forget not all His benefits: Who forgives all your iniquities, who heals all your diseases" (Psalm 103:2-3 NKJV).

God is our physician, and the medicine He prescribes is His Holy Word.

"He sent His word and healed them, and delivered them from their destructions" (Psalm 107:20 NKJV).

The Word of God heals, snatching man from the door of death.

"I am the Lord who heals you" (Exodus 15:26 NKJV).

God heals men and takes away their pains, not a physician. Yes, God may use a physician if needed, but healing comes from the Lord. And so, as Stephanie searched the net for healing, she found nothing. Praise the Lord that she finally turned to God and started praying for healing. 'God heal me,"she pleaded continually. She testified that she prayed in faith, believing that God would heal her.

"Whatever things you ask when you pray, believe that you receive them, and you will have them" (Mark 11:24 NKJV).

She knew in her heart that God would heal her. Regardless of her lousy doctor's report, symptoms, and physical pain, she had faith in God. She had child-like faith and knew God had power over the doctor's diagnosis. She continued fervently in prayer. Stephanie's continuous prayers are biblical:

"Ask, and it will be given to you; seek, and you will find; knock, and it will be opened to you" (Matthew 7:7 NKJV).

The Greek translation renders it: 'Keep on asking, keep on seeking, keep on knocking." In other words, not just once, but continually, as Stephanie did. Stephanie did not get discouraged because she prayed repeatedly. She kept going in faith, and as she kept asking, the day arrived when God did a miracle. He healed her.

Note that sometimes healing happens in layers; other times, it's instantaneous after praying once. Yet sometimes healing comes after many prayers. In Stephanie's case, HIV did not reduce gradually. It just disappeared one day after many prayers. We see Jesus demonstrating this instantaneous healing many times.

"But Jesus turned around, and when He saw her He said, "Be of good cheer, daughter; your faith has made you well." And the woman was made well from that hour" (Matthew 9:22 NKJV).

Jesus doesn't need to be standing in physical form before you to perform the same instantaneous healing today, for the Lord Jesus is still alive, and omnipresent. Jesus is with you yesterday, now, and always. His Spirit is here, there, and everywhere; and He can perform the same healings today as He did during His ministry on earth.

We must let the Lord decide how and when He will heal us: instantly or in layers. Let's trust in God and stop blaming Him for our problems. Instead, let's start making God our dwelling place, where we are safe and protected under His wing.

For, *"He who dwells in the secret place of the Most High shall abide under the shadow of the Almighty" (Psalm 91:1 NKJV).*

Turn to Him in faith and plea: *"Heal me, O Lord, and I shall be healed; save me, and I shall be saved, for You are my praise" (Jeremiah 17:14 NKJV).*

And the Lord will respond.

I NEVER KNEW GOD

Josephine's Story
I was raised as a churchgoer, attended Bible study and Sunday school, and participated in multiple church activities. Still, I didn't know God personally or have God in my heart. As I was growing up, I decided to leave the Church and take my path in life. I turned to a worldly life of drugs, drunkenness, fornication, and street life. I lived this worldly life for years.

My life was a mess, so I returned to the Church. But I still didn't know who God was. I knew about Him, but I didn't know Him personally. I learned to recite the Scriptures and I learned to speak nicely of God, but it was not the Holy Spirit speaking through me. I was only saying things I had heard all my life while going to Church. Most of what I said about God, I didn't believe in myself. I thought God's love was conditional; therefore, the Bible's portrayal of His love must be fake. I started blaming God for feeling rejected. Then I fell into depression and was upset with God.

Thankfully, church members stuck by my side, encouraging me to call out to God. I did. I cried out to God, asking Him to change my thinking. Then alone in my bedroom one day, I surrendered to God. I was honest with Him about how I was feeling. I told Him I had trouble trusting Him, was angry at Him, and blamed Him for my failed life. Then I heard a quiet voice say, "I will help you to change."

God started to show me His true character through visions, revelations, and Scripture. I began to see clearly how much He loves me and that His love is not conditional but unconditional. I experienced an unconditional love that I had never known before. I was surprised at how much God cared about everything I thought, said, and did. He cared about every aspect of my life. I am precious to Him. He is a loving Father. He assured me through Bible verses that He would never leave nor forsake me. I started to trust Him. Day by day, He led me to better myself to be more like Christ. He showed me how to change my life. God reached down into my mess and

revealed His unconditional love for me. His love changed me. He loved me when I was a sinner. He loved me when I didn't even love myself. God is faithful and is an awesome God. If you do not know God's true character let this testimony encourage you.
-Josephine Murphy

Josephine's case is a little different from the other testimonies in this book in that she got raised in church, read the Bible, recited Scripture, etc. She did all that Christian's should do, but she still turned to a worldly life. You may ask, how can one turn to a worldly life of sin after years with Christ? The answer is below:

"Whoever abides in Him does not sin. Whoever sins has neither seen Him nor known Him." (1 John 3:6 NKJV).

In other words, Josephine did Christian activities, but with one exemption: She never had God in her heart. Being religious and knowing God are two different things. For example, a religion without God makes a person cling to religion's doctrines, rituals, and institutions without knowing God personally. But to know God is to have a personal and intimate relationship with Him in your heart. A relationship with God is to know Him, to know His deep love for you, and to trust Him. It is about spending time in His presence. It is to commune with Him. The true meaning of communion is to share.

When you are in a relationship with God's Holy Spirit, you are communicating with Him, He is sharing with you, and there is a sense of communion. Understand that you can encounter God well before reading the Bible. However, an encounter with God will always lead you to the Bible.

God designed humans to need a spiritual experience with Him. When we don't have a spiritual relationship with God, we seek it out through unbiblical religions, traditions, and even carnal Christianity. In Josephine's case, she did all the religious stuff, but she did not know God in her heart. Therefore, she took the worldly path of drugs, drunkenness, fornication, and street life. God did not tell her to live a worldly lifestyle. That was her choice because she was not born again. Allow me to elaborate. Once we are saved and born again in the Spirit, we have the indwelling of the Holy Spirit. The Holy Spirit never enters a man and lets him live like the world. You can be sure of that. Once the Holy Spirit comes, it's impossible to want to do the things you used to do, to want to partake in the world, as with Josephine. The moment we partake in the worldly life, we will feel the conviction of the Holy Spirit. It is the Holy Spirit that keeps us on the straight and narrow path. He keeps us walking in the truth, the way, and the life.

Therefore, true believers abide in Christ and walk in faithful fellowship with Him, which cannot result in sin. Remember: *"Whoever abides in Him does not sin" (1 John 3:6 NKJV)*. When Christ comes into our lives and touches us, we will become a new person, living a new life without sin. A believer's life will involve some level of growth, known as sanctification, making them noticeably different from unbelievers.

However, the person whose life does not change—who shows no change from their former life nor a distinction between themselves and the unbelieving world—reveals they have not seen nor known Jesus. No one who continually sins does so because of a relationship with Christ. Every believer's life should show a noticeable difference by living a life that is in the likeness of Christ. If you continue to sin, you never knew Christ because no one can be touched by Christ and remain the same.

What we saw in Josephine's case was carnal Christianity. These are Christians who have a mental understanding of Jesus but do not know Him personally in their hearts – hypocrisy, in other words. Josephine honoured God only with her words but not with sincerity or truth.

"These people draw near to Me with their mouth, and honor Me with their lips, but their heart is far from Me" (Matthew 15:8 NKJV).

In other words, Josephine was going through the motions of religion. She put on a show by saying all the right things at the correct times but was not committed to God in her heart. She devoted herself to a religious system, not to the God the religion was meant to honor. Therefore, she knew of God but didn't know Him personally. She had no deep, intimate, loving relationship with Him.

Yes, she knew to recite Scripture, but so does Satan and many atheists know to recite. Even many theologians know the Bible word for word but do not know Jesus personally. Reciting Scripture without a relationship with God is called religion. Reciting does not mean the Holy Spirit is working in you. We see this in the Church of Sardis. Christ condemns the Church of Sardis because they had a reputation for being alive but were dead.

"And to the angel of the church in Sardis write, 'These things says He who has the seven Spirits of God and the seven stars: "I know your works, that you have a name that you are alive, but you are dead"'" (Revelation 3:1 NKJV).

Jesus is talking about the lifeless state of the Church. Some churches may have had a good reputation, but they were spiritually dead. In other words, the Church gets filled with unsaved people going through the motions of religion. Sadly, we see this in many modern-day churches, also. And through a lifeless religion, many Christians get sucked into the sinful way of life, as with Josephine.

Josephine tells how she believed that God's love was conditional, and that the love portrayed in the Bible was fake – this is being spiritually lifeless. Josephine's belief about God was a lie from the pits of hell. That was not God speaking to her. Such words can only come from the liar himself – Satan.

"He was a murderer from the beginning, and does not stand in the truth, because there is no truth in him. When he speaks a lie, he speaks from his own resources, for he is a liar and the father of it" (John 8:44 NKJV).

Believing such lies is one of many ways we give the devil a foothold. Once Josephine started believing lies about God, she began blaming Him for her wrong life choices; thus, feelings of rejection manifested. When we start dwelling on thoughts of rejection, we pave the way for the spirit of rejection to come into our lives and operate. Then the more foothold Josephine gave this unclean spirit, the more it manifested in her life. Then depression followed.

Fortunately, after the mess that Josephine made for herself in a life of drugs, drunkenness, fornication, etc., she decided to turn to Christ wholeheartedly. Her desperation made her cry out to God, asking Him to change her. Then she did a very humbling thing – she surrendered.

"Humble yourselves in the sight of the Lord, and He will lift you up" (James 4:10 NKJV).

She opened her heart to God in humility. Only then did she move from a lifeless religion to a relationship with God. Then a quiet voice said, "I will help you change." The words "I will help you" means a two-way relationship: God does His part, and Josephine does hers.

Josephine's surrender allowed the Holy Spirit to work in her freely. Then she started receiving the revelation of God's true character, His unconditional love, ultimately casting down the false imaginations of who she thought God was. God was revealing Himself through visions, revelations, and Scripture. That's what God does.

Reader, notice that Josephine first humbled herself before God, and then change came about. She did not try to approach God with pride, ego, or arrogance. Josephine did not blame God for her wrongdoings. She approached Him humbly: "Change me," she cried. She acknowledged she was powerless and turned to God for help. Therefore, her spiritual eyes opened, and she started to see clearly.

"The Lord opens the eyes of the blind; the Lord raises those who are bowed down; the Lord loves the righteous" (Psalm 146:8 NKJV).

Once the demonic veil of deceit got removed from her eyes through surrender to God, she could see God's unconditional love for her. As revelations kept coming in, God built her trust in Him using Scripture. She was becoming more like Christ. God was changing her. She testified, "God's love changed me."

"I will sing of mercy and justice; to You, O Lord, I will sing praises. I will behave wisely in a perfect way. Oh, when will You come to me? I will walk within my house with a perfect heart. I will set nothing wicked before my eyes; I hate the work of those who fall away; it shall not cling to me. A perverse heart shall depart from me; I will not know wickedness" (Psalm 101:1-4 NKJV).

FROM ISLAM TO JESUS

Abdullah's Story
I was an Islamic terrorist arrested in Pakistan for carrying illegal passports. Thrown into an Islamic prison, I sat in my cell, meditating on the verses of the Quran. Suddenly the evil presence of a spirit was there. It filled me with the fear that my life was in danger. I started rebuking the demon in the name of Allah. In my native language, I shouted, "Allah, help me," but nothing happened.

Then I heard a voice saying, "Call the Name of Jesus." Without thinking, I said, "Jesus, if You are true, show me Yourself." And instantly, the demon was gone. Then I felt a holy presence enter my atmosphere. The first thing I knew about this God was that He was holy. I became supernaturally aware that he was holy and just, and that He would righteously judge my sins.

I felt a touch on my shoulder, and heard a voice that said, "I forgive you." I cried and said, 'Who are You that forgives me?" And He said, "I am the way, the truth, and the life." I didn't understand that because I had never heard those words before. I asked, "What is your name?" He said, "Jesus Christ." I fell to the floor and wept. The next day, I told fellow prisoners what had happened; some mocked me, and others followed me in faith in Jesus Christ.
- Abdullah Abad

Reader, In Abdullah's case, we see the presence of many demon spirits operating in his life long before he was arrested and sent to prison. We see the spirit of religion, terror, murder, and the antichrist spirit. These are very dangerous demon spirits. Let's look at each one individually.

The Spirit of Religion
According to Abdullah's testimony, he got involved in the religion of Islam. Reader, is God the same god in all religions? I've heard this question asked many times, so let's examine what the Bible says.

Jesus said, *"I am the way, the truth, and the life. No one comes to the Father except through Me" (John 14:6 NKJV).*

All religions do not lead to God. Any teaching that does not point to Christ as the only path to God the Father is a false religion. The spirit operating behind this erroneous doctrine is the religious spirit. A religious spirit is a demonic spirit that influences a person, or group of people, to replace a genuine relationship with God with religion – in Abdullah's case, it's Islam. Even if you sincerely worship the gods of other religions, you're not honoring the one true God revealed in Jesus Christ. The Bible tells us that the gods of other religions besides Christianity are in opposition to the one true God.

The spirit of religion loves to be worshiped and wants to deceive the world and take the place of the true God. In addition, this spirit can open the door for terrorism to enter a person's life. For this reason, religious terrorists are primarily motivated by religion.

The Spirit of Terror
The spirit of terror is behind terrorism. "Terror" in the word "terrorism" means extreme fear. "Ism" in the word "terrorism" means to practice. In other words, behind terrorism is a demon who practices terror by inflicting extreme fear on its victims. The spirit of terror uses murder as one of its tactics to inflict terror and fear.

The Spirit of Murder
A terrorist is a vessel of darkness who justifies killing. Murder is a sin that violates God's principles, for the Bible commands, *"You shall not murder" (Exodus 20:13 NKJV).*

The Antichrist Spirit
The antichrist spirit is an unclean spirit that teaches false doctrines that oppose Jesus Christ, substituting itself in Christ's place. Therefore, any teaching that does not have Biblical Christ as the center is not a teaching from God.

The Apostle Paul stated, *"But even if we, or an angel from heaven, preach any other gospel to you than what we have preached to you, let him be accursed"* (Galatians 1:8 NKJV).

If the gospel is modified, adjusted, or changed by anyone for any reason, it is no longer the true gospel; thus, this person is a curse. Muslims reject the Christian gospel, which they say is not the original teachings of Jesus, but a teaching that got corrupted over time. They speak of a different Jesus than the Jesus of the Holy Bible. They claim that Jesus was not crucified, nor was He raised from the dead, nor is He the Saviour of the world, etc. Reader, the Jesus of the Quran is not the real Jesus.

"Beloved, do not believe every spirit, but test the spirits, whether they are of God; because many false prophets have gone out into the world. By this you know the Spirit of God: Every spirit that confesses that Jesus Christ has come in the flesh is of God, and every spirit that does not confess that Jesus Christ has come in the flesh is not of God. And this is the spirit of the Antichrist, which you have heard was coming, and is now already in the world" (1 John 4:1-3 NKJV).

We are to test the spirits because the presence of false teachers is growing. Truth only comes from the Holy Spirit.

"When He, the Spirit of truth, has come, He will guide you into all truth" (John 16:13 NKJV).

Everything else comes from evil. Therefore, it is essential to have a way to test which teachers and leaders are from God. Below are multiple ways to test them.

1. When a person confesses Jesus is Christ and that Jesus came fully human and fully God into the world, such a person has the Holy Spirit. But when people or religions deny that Jesus was fully human and fully God, such people or religions are of an antichrist spirit. The Bible tells us that Jesus is God who came from heaven to earth in tangible, physical, and human form.

"In the beginning was the Word, and the Word was with God, and the Word was God" (John 1:1 NKJV).

In other words, Jesus is the Word of God and is God Himself. Then the Bible tells us, *"And the Word became flesh and dwelt among us" (John 1:14 NKJV).*

In other words, Jesus, who is God, took on human form and walked the earth. Thus, if people or religions deny that Jesus walked the earth as both God and fully human, they deny the identity of Jesus; therefore, they are false teachers and have an antichrist spirit.

"For many deceivers have gone out into the world who do not confess Jesus Christ as coming in the flesh. This is a deceiver and an antichrist (2 John 1:7 NKJV).

Those who reject the biblical Jesus are against Christ, and therefore, antichrists.

2. Anyone rejecting Christ's literal, bodily resurrection is a false teacher and has an antichrist spirit.

"He is not here, but is risen! Remember how He spoke to you when He was still in Galilee, saying, 'The Son of Man must be delivered into the hands of sinful men, and be crucified, and the third day rise again.'" (Luke 24:6-7 NKJV).

A woman came to honor Jesus in His death, but an angel spoke to her, saying that He was no longer dead.

Jesus said, *"I am He who lives, and was dead, and behold, I am alive forevermore" (Revelation 1:18 NKJV).*

Jesus is alive. He died, but death could not hold Him. He arose and is alive forever. Denial of His resurrection comes from an antichrist spirit.

3. If a person confesses Jesus as Lord, they have publicly professed to become a Christian. Such a person has a godly spirit. But if a person refuses to confess Jesus is Christ, that person is not of God.

"Who is a liar but he who denies that Jesus is the Christ? He is antichrist who denies the Father and the Son" (1 John 2:22 NKJV).

Such false teachers who do not confess Christ are the spirit of the antichrist. Sadly, many religions promote this antichrist doctrine. Their teachings promote a phony godliness that exists apart from the biblical Jesus.

"Having a form of godliness but denying its power. And from such people turn away!" (2 Timothy 3:5 NKJV).

Religions that appear as faith in God but reject the power of the Holy Spirit are indicative of rejecting the will and wisdom of God. Reader, Abdullah had an antichrist spirit; thus, he was a vessel of darkness. His walking in darkness led to his arrest. In prison, he began meditating on the Quran. He testifies that he immediately felt an evil presence in his prison cell, filling him with fear.

Fear is an unclean spirit, for *"God has not given us a spirit of fear, but of power and of love and of a sound mind" (2 Timothy 1:7 NKJV).*

The spirit of fear and death that Abdullah inflicted through terrorism backfired and now affected him. Reader, do not get deceived. You can't escape the demons that you open doors to, for once they enter your life, they don't leave unless Jesus comes in and sets you free. That's why nothing happened when Abdullah started rebuking the demon in Allah's name. Demons recognize and submit only to the authority of Jesus, not of Allah, Buddha, Lord Shiva, nor of any other name.

Jesus said, *"All authority has been given to Me in heaven and on earth" (Matthew 28:18 NKJV).*

Demons obey Jesus, and believers of Jesus have the authority to execute Jesus's power.

"Then the seventy returned with joy, saying, *"Lord, even the demons are subject to us in Your name" (Luke 10:17 NKJV).*

Abdullah testifies that with the demon of fear still present in his prison cell, he heard a still voice telling him to call on the Name of Jesus. He obeyed, saying, "Jesus, if You are true, show me Yourself." Immediately the demon was gone, which tells us Jesus was present in Abdullah's prison cell. The demon had to leave, for demons' flea at Jesus's command.

"There was a man in their synagogue with an unclean spirit. And he cried out, saying, 'Let us alone! What have we to do with You, Jesus of Nazareth? Did You come to destroy us? I know who You are—the Holy One of God!' But Jesus rebuked him, saying, 'Be quiet, and come out of him!' And when the unclean spirit had convulsed him and cried out with a loud voice, he came out of him" (Mark 1:23-26 NKJV).

Time and time again, the Bible tells us that demons flee at Jesus's command. When the presence of Jesus entered Abdullah's prison cell, the demon left. Abdullah then felt a touch on his shoulder, and a voice said, "I forgive you." "Who are You that You forgive me?" replied Abdullah. "I am Jesus," answer the still voice. Abdullah was instantly transformed into a new man. Reader, no one can be touched by Jesus and remain the same. When Jesus comes into your life, He will change you from the inside out. One touch by Jesus, and your life changes forever.

Notice that it was not until Abdullah called upon the Name Jesus that Jesus entered his prison cell, forced the demon to leave, and turned Abdullah into a new man. Reader, if Jesus did it for Abdullah, He can do it for you, also. Call upon the Name of the Lord, Jesus Christ, and be saved.

"Bless the Lord, O my soul; and all that is within me, bless His holy name! Bless the Lord, O my soul, and forget not all His benefits: Who forgives all your iniquities, who heals all your diseases, who redeems your life from destruction, who crowns you with lovingkindness and tender mercies, who satisfies your mouth with good things, so that your youth is renewed like the eagle's. The Lord executes righteousness and justice for all who are oppressed. He made known His ways to Moses, His acts to the children of Israel. The Lord is merciful and gracious, slow to anger, and abounding in mercy" (Psalm 103:1-8 NKJV).

WHEN A CHILD'S SOUL GETS SHATTERED THROUGH ABUSE

Mahsa's Story
One month after my birth in Iran, my parents died in an earthquake. I was found buried under heaps of ruins and taken to an orphanage. I was adopted at the age of four by a married couple. Shortly after, my foster dad married a second woman, who hated me. At six years old, my foster dad started sexually abusing me with the knowledge of his wives. As a result of the rape, I became his third wife at age ten. Every third night it was my turn to have sex with him.

Fear and anxiety took over my life. I cried myself to sleep every night. I couldn't understand how someone could be so cruel. I was accused by his other wives that I had stolen their husband, so they hated me. I got threatened to keep the abuse silent, or the police would arrest me and send me to jail. Every day they starved me. I stole food to survive.

When my foster dad/ husband gave me money for school, I had to repay him with sex. They repeatedly threatened me and beat me until they drew blood. "We hope you die," they told me often. I could not understand how they could be so mean. At eleven, my foster dad sold me for sex to his friend. I wanted to die. When I was old enough, I left the house. I remarried and had two beautiful children.

One day, I felt this nudge in my heart to call out to Jesus. I prayed, "Jesus, please help me." I got saved and started to follow Jesus Christ. Jesus began to heal my soul from the old wounds. After some time, He healed me completely. Jesus freed me of all the tormenting things of the past. He taught me how to love, forgive and move on. I was finally free. Then the Spirit led me to share my testimony of how Jesus healed and set me free.

I encourage you that Jesus saves, Jesus heals, and Jesus delivers. He has risen from the dead and is alive. Turn to Him, and He will save

you. Don't endure your suffering for years as I did. Call upon Jesus now and let Him heal and deliver you.
-Mahsa

In Mahsa's case, we see Iranian origin, which implies an Islamic background, which means the family was not under the authoritative head of Jesus Christ; therefore, were not covered by the protective blood of Jesus. Islam is a religion centered primarily around the Quran, a religious text that Muslims consider to be the direct word of God. We know this to be false because Jesus is the living Word of God.

"In the beginning was the Word, and the Word was with God, and the Word was God. He was in the beginning with God" (John 1:1-2 NKJV).

Jesus was at the beginning with God; He is the Word of God, and Jesus is God. Anything other than this teaching is a false view of truth. We see the spirit of error operating in Mahsa's family, inflicting flaws, delusion, and corruption in their thinking. Due to the spirit of error, the demon of religion, and other unclean spirits, Mahsa's family was open to demonic influence. For example, evil activity operating through the foster dad as he molests Mahsa.

Parents have parental authority to close those demonic doors and keep the child covered by the protective blood of Jesus. But as the foster parents were not operating under the authoritative head of Jesus Christ, they could not act as a protective covering for the child; for they, too, were in demonic bondage. Mahsa's foster parents were ignorantly operating as vessels of darkness, beating Mahsa until she bled. Often declaring to her, "We hope you die." This transference from parent to child made Mahsa an open target for evil to enter her life. We read that the spirit of fear took over her life, leading to anxiety, and destructive thinking.

Mahsa testified her life was constantly threatened and tormented – here we see signs of the tormenting spirit operating in her life. As demons pave the way for the next unclean spirit to come in, and with her foster parents declaring death over her, the path got paved for the spirit of murder to come into Mahsa's life. Finally, Mahsa gave in. Tormented and threatened, she wanted to die – that was the spirit of murder in operation. When Mahsa spoke, "I want to die," she entered an agreement with the murdering spirit, that comes to kill. Reader, are you beginning to understand how unclean spirits enter people's lives, even from childhood?

In adulthood, Mahsa felt a call in her heart to relocate. She obeyed the prompt. In her new location she remarried, and God blessed her with kids. But the question is: "Who nudged Mahsa to relocate?" That was the Holy Spirit, of course. Then Mahsa felt another nudge in her heart to call out to Jesus. Again, that was the Holy Spirit. Again, she obeyed. "Jesus, help me," she prayed.

The Bible promises: *"Whoever calls on the name of the Lord shall be saved" (Romans 10:13 NKJV).*

Mahsa got immediately saved. She started following Jesus, and He began healing her from the inside out: wounds, soul, traumas, everything. She was set free from the tormenting spirit, the spirit of murder, the spirit of fear, and more. "I was healed completely," she testified. Jesus taught her to forgive those who hurt her and to love others genuinely without conditions. Hallelujah!

Note that the Holy Spirit who nudged Mahsa to relocate and to call on the Name Jesus is the same Holy Spirit who continuously leads everyone through life, even before they come to faith in Christ. Then each person has free will to obey the lead of God's Spirit or to rebel. Those who rebel reject Christ. Those who accept and come to Christ get saved, and the whole transformation process begins. Reader, if Jesus can do it for Mahsa, He can do it for you, also.

"The righteous cry out, and the Lord hears, and delivers them out of all their trouble" (Psalm 34:17 NKJV).

I SAW THE HAND OF GOD

My Story
Alcoholics and fortune-tellers were in my family history. I frequently had my fortune told by my grandmother and aunties, and I secretly had my first alcoholic drink at 13 years old. I ran away from home at the age of fifteen. Mixing with the wrong crowds, I got into alcohol and marijuana use daily. At seventeen, I got sexually abused. I was a heroin addict at nineteen. At twenty, I was arrested and faced with a five-year prison sentence. At twenty-one, I woke up in the hospital with facial and head injuries due to a severe car accident; that's when I contemplated suicide. I had a drug overdose at twenty-three.

Addicted and rebellious, I became homeless in London at twenty-four, where I slept on street corners and waste areas. A ghetto with high unemployment, high crime rates, and inadequate municipality services was my home for two years. Street life led to shoplifting, which got me arrested and sent to prison. Upon my release, I wanted to stop the drugs, so I turned to the bottle. This begun a six-year battle with alcoholism and dark depression. That's when I started thinking about suicide more. I began to live life constantly at deaths door.

One night, I mixed two handfuls of sleeping pills with a large bottle of whisky and began to drink. I woke up in the hospital feeling depressed and hopeless. From then onward, I lived in a state of panic. I couldn't eat or sleep. Anxiety became my everyday life. I felt I was slowly deteriorating.

I got into new age spirituality for answers and solutions, which brought witchcraft into my life. Due to the new age practices, my surroundings started to feel evil, and I constantly battled with physical health issues and demonic attacks. I couldn't understand how new age practices promised peace and freedom, yet they caused me to feel more trapped and tormented.

Late one summer night, as I lay on my bed, I looked up at the ceiling while my mind searched for answers. Almost by a supernatural force, I felt a strong urge to speak the following words:

"I don't know who you are, what you are, or where you are, but I need to know the truth, whatever that truth is."

And that's when it happened! An intense, transparent, bright, white light immediately appeared and flooded the room.

"Now it happened, as I journeyed and came near Damascus at about noon, suddenly a great light from heaven shone around me" (Acts 22:6 NKJV).

The white light was so bright yet so comfortable to the eyes. It was a white whiter than any white I have ever seen. Such a white does not exist on planet Earth. This white light penetrated every part of my being. Simultaneously, I found myself in a peaceful state filled with unconditional love – something I had never experienced before. That was my first encounter with Jesus Christ. Full awareness of His presence filled me. His company was so intense and so real.

The love and peace of Jesus Christ entered my soul and crowded out depression and anguish. All the exhaustion had fled and in its place was vitality and life. I witnessed a miracle right then — I got transformed in an instant. I lost my lonesomeness and feelings of fear; I felt new. In one instance, I was healed from depression, addiction, and anxiety. Every demon, curse, and witchcraft faded into nothingness. Jesus brought me peace and love, and I had rest for the first time in my soul. When I opened my eyes after three hours, I could see. Something like invisible scales fell from my eyes, and I could see.

"Immediately there fell from his eyes something like scales, and he received his sight at once" (Acts 9:18 NKJV).

Then I saw the light ascending back to heaven. Immediately I noticed I was a changed woman. My atmosphere changed from evil to love.

"The light shines in the darkness, and the darkness has not overcome it" (John 1:5 NKJV).

Reader, I saw the hand of God upon my life. He stepped in and rescued me from the darkness that surrounded me. He snatched me out of the pits of evil, broke every addiction, depression, anxiety, and witchcraft, and freed me from the bondage of sin. Jesus has completely transformed everything inside me and everything outside of me. I am free because of Christ. Then I got baptized and gave my life to Jesus. Now I live for Christ, my King.
-Venetia Zannettis (Author of this book)

Reader, the testimony shared above is my life story. From a young age, many demon spirits were operating in my life and family. There was a generational curse of alcohol addiction and witchcraft. There also was a generational curse of divination, passed down from my great-grandmother to my grandmother, aunties, cousins, and then to me. Divination is a serious offense, a severe violation of God's rules.

"There shall not be found among you anyone who makes his son or his daughter pass through the fire, or one who practices witchcraft, or a soothsayer, or one who interprets omens, or a sorcerer, or one who conjures spells, or a medium, or a spiritist, or one who calls up the dead" (Deuteronomy 18:10-11 NKJV).

The Bible instructs us to stay far away from such people. Divination invokes unclean spirits, bringing demonization in many cases. When a family or person has an ancestral sin of divination, expect curses and illnesses to be passed down from one generation to another.

"Visiting the iniquity of the fathers upon the children and the children's children to the third and the fourth generation" (Exodus 34:7 NKJV).

In other words, my family was paying for the sins of our ancestors because we had not yet let Jesus into our lives to break that family curse.

While we are not responsible for the sins of our ancestors, we are affected by them when we permit them to continue; thus, the curse of divination, witchcraft, and addiction prolonged, destroying my household. Due to a cursed family tree, I began to show signs of a rebellious nature at a very young age. Thus, together with the spirit of divination, rebellion was also operating in my life. When the spirit of rebellion enters a person's life, that individual will resist all forms of authority: family, government, school, church, etc. In essence, I was rebelling against God.

The Bible says, *"Rebellion is as the sin of witchcraft" (1 Samuel 15:23 NKJV)*.

Practicing witchcraft is a severe sin according to God, and a rebellious person is just as sinful as a person who practices witchcraft. Rebellion is the spirit of witchcraft. As I rose in opposition, I opened the door of my heart to all sorts of unclean spirits: the spirit of addiction, the spirit of fear, and the spirit of murder, to name a few.

Since alcohol addiction was already in my family tree, dependency lurked. Influenced by the spirit of rebellion, addiction knocked, and I opened. Then drugs and alcohol became my full-time occupation; thus, my soul was drenched deep in addiction.

Many people say stimulant drugs can make you depressed, anxious, and paranoid. I say differently: Stimulant drugs open doors for demons to come in and influence feelings of depression, anxiety, and paranoia.

As my mind got hijacked through mind-altering drugs, the devil whispered lies into my mind: "Your life is not worth living." "You must fear." "There is no hope." And that's when the spirit of murder entered my life, feeding me the lie: "Suicide will bring relief." Emotionally unstable through the spirit of divination and mentally sluggish due to drug and alcohol abuse, I attempted suicide with pills and alcohol in the front room of my apartment. The devil came to kill me (John 10:10). It is by the grace of God that I am alive today to give this testimony.

Reader, please understand that unless Jesus comes in and sets us free, we will continue to go from one addiction to the next, never breaking the dependence, but only substituting the substances. Understand that there are no multiple addictions: drugs, alcohol, cigarettes, gambling, sex, work, etc. There is only one addiction – the spirit of addiction. Everything else is a manifestation of that demon. In other words, the problem is not drugs, alcohol, gambling, etc. The problem is the spirit of addiction.

Therefore, unless Jesus comes into our lives and casts out that unclean spirit, we will always move from one addiction to the next. We will only substitute the substance for another substance, but the curse of addiction will not break. For example, I quit heroin addiction and turned to cocaine addiction. Then I left cocaine addiction and turned to alcohol addiction. Some people stop cocaine and turn to sex addiction. Others quit cigarette addiction and start food addiction, or vice versa: stopping food and starting cigarette addiction. Understand that the spirit of addiction enslaves people, not the substance itself. Without the spirit of addiction operating in our lives, we would not be addicted to x, y, z.

Due to spirits of divination, addiction, fear, and murder, my life became depressive. Depression is not a demon. It's normal to feel depressed due to painful or traumatic life experiences. However, when depression is chronic, causing thoughts of suicide or feelings of hopelessness or apathy – that depression is now demonically influenced.

Influenced by demons, my deception ran high. That's when I got deceived into new-age spirituality; thus, I ignorantly opened more doors to witchcraft. Through new age practices and rituals, I got tormented – that was the first sign of the tormenting spirit in my life.

It was not until I surrendered and called out for the truth that Jesus came. Is it not surprising that I called out for truth, and Jesus came?

Jesus said, *"I am the way, the **truth**, and the life. No one comes to the Father except through Me" (John 14:6 NKJV).*

Upon calling Jesus, peace came upon me. *"For unto us a Child is born, and His name will be called Wonderful, Counselor, Mighty God, Everlasting Father, **Prince of Peace**" (Isaiah 9:6).*

Simultaneously unconditional love entered my life. *"God is love" (1 John 4:8 NKJV).*

God entered my life, and immediately all darkness got destroyed. *"For this purpose the Son of God was manifested, that He might destroy the works of the devil" (1 John 3:8 NKJV).*

Jesus set me free. *"If the Son makes you free, you shall be free indeed" (John 8:36 NKJV).*

He transformed me in an instant. I was made new. *"If anyone is in Christ, he is a new creation; old things have passed away; behold, all things have become new" (2 Corinthians 5:17 NKJV).*

Hallelujah, this is the grace of God!

"But God, who is rich in mercy, because of His great love with which He loved us, even when we were dead in trespasses, made us alive together with Christ (by grace you have been saved)" (Ephesians 2:4-5 NKJV).

THE SPIRIT OF THIS WORLD

As is evident from the testimonies shared, there is much evil and suffering in this world. This is due to people living in sin and rebelling against God. We live in a self-absorbed world that encourages its citizens to reject God and trust only themselves. There is a spirit that is in operation in this world, responsible for the world's chaos. The spirit of this world is Satan.

He is *"the spirit who is now at work in those who are disobedient" (Ephesians 2:2 NIV).*

Satan is a spirit, not a human, who works in the lives of those who disobey God – unbelievers who live worldly.

"For all that is in the world—the lust of the flesh, the lust of the eyes, and the pride of life—is not of the Father but is of the world" (1 John 2:15 NKJV).

Worldliness is not of God but of the evil one. The "term world" refers to the fallen, man-centered system or way of life. It is the fallen nature of man that rejects God. This creates a godless world system of humanity, culture, and beliefs which repudiates God and His authority. Worldliness is a world system headed by Satan, designed to leave God out. In other words, it is a system where Satan diligently gets humankind to exclude God from the equation. It's all about getting people to sin, to lust, get prideful, and covet. Thus, people get mentally conditioned to chase money, fame, status, and success. They do whatever it takes to get what they want out of life. They believe they are their own source of provision and are willing to manipulate and fight to meet their demands. It's an ungodly world influenced by Satan.

Someone who loves how this world operates, including its control by sin, is a person who cannot focus on the Father's will. In other words, they cannot truly love God because there is a contrast between the love of the world and the love of the Father. Jesus offered an example of this contrast when Satan tempted Him in the wilderness.

"The devil took Him up on an exceedingly high mountain, and showed Him all the kingdoms of the world and their glory. And he said to Him, 'All these things I will give You if You will fall down and worship me.' Then Jesus said to him, 'Away with you, Satan! For it is written, "You shall worship the Lord your God, and Him only you shall serve "'" (Matthew 4:10 NKJV).

Beware: some dangers will befall those who start to love this world and the things of this world. One cannot love this world system and its things and love God simultaneously, for the whole structure of this world system is opposite from the ways of God. Loving the world and its ways is incompatible with our love for the Father and His desire for our lives.

The world and all that it offers can appear enticing and not harmful, but that's a deception. Its design seduces our senses and stimulates our fleshly desires into an ungodly, selfish, and addictive appetite, which craves more ungodliness. These are the lusts of the flesh, which seduce our selfish wants. The lust of the eyes refers to the craving and coveting of the things we see. And the pride of life refers to humankind's self-interest, self-indulgence, self-importance, self-love, self-glorification, self-reliance, and self-righteousness. In addition, we have self-deification, making ourselves gods. All this lust and pride is how humanity gets enticed away from God into a carnal reliance on the things of this world.

Man gets drawn away from a spiritual walk, where Christ reigns, to a fleshly existence where the "self" replaces God. By doing so, we choke the spiritual communication channel between man and God; thus, God is not felt, heard, nor experienced. Therefore, the destruction in this world is because most of humanity does not allow God to reign in their lives. They do not want to make God the head of their lives. People choose to reject Christ and live a worldly life because they love sin.

Understand that this is not a godforsaken world. It is a world that has forsaken God. Then humankind blames God for their problems when most of their problems come from not listening to God. Humankind chooses to follow the ways of this world, ignorant of the fact that they follow Satan. That's why the world is so much in conflict with God's ways and unknowingly following Satan. Thus, the world has a hostility toward God.

"The Spirit of truth, whom the world cannot receive, because it neither sees Him nor knows Him" (John 14:17 NKJV).

Unlike the spirit of this world, who is Satan, the Spirit of Truth is the Holy Spirit, who dwells in those who come to Christ. Those who do not come to Christ do not have God's Holy Spirit in them. The people who reject Christ don't see Christ, so they neither see God, nor know God. Instead, they blindly follow the spirit of this world, drowning in worldliness, completely lost in sin. Due to their sinful way of life, sinful people reject Christ because He uncovers the darkness that is in man. He unmasks who they are. And the perfection of Jesus exposes their imperfection.

"The world cannot hate you, but it hates Me because I testify of it that its works are evil" (John 7:7 NKJV).

The world does not hate those who are in the image of the world because they are a part of the world, under the influence of the world. But it hates Jesus because He makes known the evil in the world. The dark world does not like to get exposed for what it does; and because Christ's ministry confronts sin and hypocrisy, the world hates Him. Sadly, man's typical response to conviction is not repentance, but hatred and violence. They willingly choose worldliness because they love sin.

But, *"Do you not know that friendship with the world is enmity with God? Whoever therefore wants to be a friend of the world makes himself an enemy of God" (James 4:4 NKJV).*

When unbelievers choose to live according to this world, they essentially cheat on God with the world; for this, Apostle James called them adulterers.

We can't be friends both with the world and with God. Anyone who continues to be friends with the world is living as God's enemy. People who choose to live according to the world, driven by envy and ambition, seeking what they want above all else, are not living as friends of God.

Therefore, the Bible warns, *"Do not love the world or the things in the world. If anyone loves the world, the love of the Father is not in him" (1 john 2:15 NKJV).*

By loving how this world operates, its possessions, and its control by sin, we cannot be focused on God, nor can we love God with all our hearts. Understand that there is a contrast between the love of the world and the love of the Father. Therefore, it is crucial to overcome the world and its sinful patterns. Instead, we must love the Lord our God with all our heart, and with all our soul, and with all our mind, and all our strength. It is necessary to overcome the world and seek to walk in Spirit and truth, to His praise and glory. Be like Jesus, who gave Satan no advantage over Him.

"The ruler of this world is coming, and he has nothing in Me" (John 14:30 NKJV).

The "ruler of this world" refers to Satan, who comes to people, influencing them into sin, just as he came to betray Jesus through Judas. But Jesus said, "Satan has nothing in Me." No hold, claim, power, control, authority, or accusation. Satan has nothing over Jesus. And that's why we need Jesus and His reign and protection over us. Otherwise, Satan, who has direct involvement in the world through his influence over humans, will blind our minds to the truth that is Christ.

"Whose minds the god of this age has blinded, who do not believe, lest the light of the gospel of the glory of Christ, who is the image of God, should shine on them" (2 Corinthians 4:4 NKJV).

Satan aims to keep those perishing from coming to Christ and being freed. Satan has influence over the world, not because he is powerful, but because people ignorantly give him power, and because they love sin. Thus, the devil actively blinds the minds of those who don't believe in Jesus, keeping them from coming to faith in Christ. His purpose is to keep them from seeing the light. The veil that blinds the minds of unbelievers gets removed once a person turns to God in faith. Only then can man see God's glory and begin to be transformed to become more like Jesus. Otherwise, men will continue to perish. They do not understand the truth of Christ because they refuse to understand.

Therefore, I urge you, *"Do not be conformed to this world, but be transformed by the renewing of your mind, that you may prove what is that good and acceptable and perfect will of God"* (Romans 12:2 NKJV).

I encourage you to get out of worldliness. No longer be conformed to the world's system, the desires of the sinful flesh, the pride of life, the things you chase in pursuit of false happiness, nor the way that every human being lives by default. Abandon the chase for pleasure, idolizing possessions, and stop living sinfully.

Instead, respond to God's mercy, forgiveness of your sin, and invitation to enter His family. Offer your life to Him and dedicate it to His ways. Allow Christ to change how you think and be transformed from the inside out. Have your mind renewed so that you can begin to understand what God's will for your life is. Do it for His purposes and not for your selfish appetites. I encourage you to snap out of the worldly view, for this world is not the basis on which you must live and operate. Come out from the darkness, stop rebelling against God, and enter the Kingdom of God, which gives life.

I am not saying to withdraw from the world, for as believers, we are expected to be in the world but not of the world. Otherwise, we cannot bring the truth to those who need to hear it. If we withdraw from the world, we cannot be present, engaging the people around us, drawing them out of darkness and into the light of Christ. Can you see why we must be in this world but not part of the world system?

You must walk as *"blameless and harmless, children of God without fault in the midst of a crooked and perverse generation, among whom you shine as lights in the world"* (Philippians 2:15 NKJV).

Live in a way explicitly different from the depraved world in which you live. Through Christ, you can overcome difficult situations and temptations and stand out as a unique and powerful example – that's how to be the light in this dark world.

"Let your light shine before others, so that they may see your good works and give glory to your Father who is in heaven" (Matthew 5:16 NIV).

Can you see how life with God differs from the worldly life? God asks us to trust in Him to provide all we need. And because God provides, we don't have to abuse each other to get what we want. Instead, we obey God, love genuinely, serve each other, and help meet each other's needs. God wants us to overcome the world and walk in the example of Jesus, setting for others the governing guidelines and regulations for how to live life. In other words, we must live by God's rules in every area of life.

God must get recognized as the comprehensive Ruler of our lives. There must be no area of life where God's view is not brought in and acted on. We must start to see life in agreement with God, functioning as God designed us to perform. We must return to His plan, authority, rule, and government. Unless God is free to call the shots, the transformation we need in our lives and this world will not happen. If God does not get treated as God, we will continue to live in a broken world; thus, we will never see Him put together what we have broken. Reader, that's the only way to survive in this world and see the victory, power, and provision that God is offering us.

When we begin to operate in God's realm, we will influence all we touch and finally see change. We shall see God take messes and turn them into miracles. We will see Him take circumstances and reverse them. But first we must come to Christ, the only One who can set us free from the yoke of slavery that entangles the world.

JESUS CHRIST OUR SAVIOUR

It is evident from the testimonies shared in this book that all who come to Jesus get saved, healed, and delivered. Not some, but all. We see the same happen during Christ's ministry on earth.

"They brought to Him many who were demon-possessed; and He cast out the spirits with a word, and healed all who were ill" (Matthew 18:16 NKJV).

Understand that it's not normal to have sickness, live in oppression, be bound by addiction, or suffer suicidal thoughts. It's not normal. These are not the works of God but the evil one. But Jesus came to set the captives free. Jesus is the miracle worker who can take an addict, a murderer, a thief, a prostitute, a homeless person, or a leper and turn their life around. It is clear from the testimonies that Jesus came to people during their darkest moments and turned their lives around.

He came to me alone in my bedroom, bound by unclean spirits and new-age witchcraft, and set me free. Jesus went to a suicidal man in his prison cell and set him free. Jesus went to a woman while she lay sick on a hospital bed and healed her. Jesus will come to you where you are: in prison, in hospital, with depression or dementia, or insanity. He will come on that street corner where you sit homeless. He will come while you lay drunk in your vomit.

He will send His messengers into prison to save the lost souls behind bars. He may come personally to find you, lying on your bed in depression. Or He can use people, visions, Scriptures, dreams, YouTube videos, or even this book to save you. Jesus cannot be limited to location, time, or mental state. He will come to find you wherever you are. Jesus will knock on the door of your heart, and when you open it for Him, He will come in. Then Jesus will save, deliver, and heal you of all infirmities and situations. Afterward, He will use your struggles and your testimony of deliverance for His glory. Hallelujah!

Reader, the salvation, deliverance, and healing that has happened to thousands of thousands worldwide can also happen to you. You, too, can walk in the light after being in so much darkness all your life. You, too, can be free from the web of witchcraft that only entangles you deeper. You, too, can have life after walking in perpetual death – this is the grace of God. God will never give up on you. Therefore, be reassured that Jesus can save you in your current situation, for no one is too lost that God cannot find them. No one is too addicted that God cannot set them free, nor too insane that God cannot bring back sanity, nor too broken that He cannot restore.

Reader, this is God's grace, *"for the grace of God that brings salvation has appeared to all men" (Titus 2:11 NKJV).*

God saves, delivers, and heals all people. At the same time, He knows the lengths we must go through to recover us, and He will permit us to go there, even to the darkest corners of the world. This darkness is on the brink of complete physical, moral, and spiritual poverty for some people. For other people, it's a place where everyone has turned their backs on them. Yet, for others, it's a near-death experience. It is in these darkest times that we seek God. Therefore, He permits the destruction of the false ideologies we create for ourselves so that He can give us an actual reality in Christ. And so, even when God allows you to reach desperation, it is so that you can cling to Him even more and learn to grow through challenges, maturing into a Christ-like image.

Therefore, have faith that *"Even if you have been banished to the most distant land under the heavens, from there the Lord your God will gather you and bring you back" (Deuteronomy 30:4 NKJV).*

Call upon the Lord Jesus Christ; then trust Him, even when your senses and logic seem to suggest the opposite or appear to contradict His promised truth. Let your heart be oriented toward God. Allow His Holy Spirit to be magnified in you as a magnifying glass magnifies a speck, and His Holy Spirit will work prominently in you. Give Him your soul so He can think through your mind and feel through your heart. He will use your mind, body, and spirit to work love through you, casting out demons, lifting oppression, and healing all sicknesses, because *"where the Spirit of the Lord is, there is liberty" (2 Corinthians 3:17 NKJV)*.

Therefore, choose Christ and let go of your old life. Don't be like those who continue to walk in darkness because they shut Jesus out of their lives. Entrust Him with everything that hurts you. Don't keep anything back. Understand that Satan doesn't want you to be redeemed and set free from your pain; so if you reveal all your suffering to Jesus, the enemy no longer has power over you to torment you with past hurts; thus you can recover. A common misconception is that you must clean up and fix your life before coming to God. That's a lie. The truth is that you come to God, and He will change you. He will make you a brand new person.

"Then He who sat on the throne said, 'Behold, I make all things new'" (Revelation 21:5 NKJV).

Jesus is the One who makes you brand new, bringing transformation to your life. Jesus is He who saves lost souls, sets free from sin, heals the sick, breaks bondages, and lifts oppression. It is through Jesus that man is born again and given new life in the likeness of God.

His Name is Jesus Christ of Nazareth, and He is the Saviour of this dark world. He existed before His physical birth, coming down to a world that He created to save humankind from eternal damnation due to sin. He came and took the world's sins, diseases, and infirmities on His body and crucified them. When Jesus's physical body died, the world's sins, illnesses, and infirmities died too. All suicidal thoughts, depression, anxiety, fear, insomnia, cancer, and aids got crucified with Jesus on the cross. All demonic bondages, witchcraft, and oppression died too.

Jesus used His physical body to put the world's evil to death by crucifixion, defeating the works of the devil. In other words, His body was the vehicle through which all forms of wickedness got buried.

Then Jesus rose from the dead, defeating death itself. Reader, the cross was a victory, not a defeat. The resurrection was a sign of Christ's victory over the powers of darkness that kept man influenced by sin and evil.

"He himself bore our sins" in his body on the cross, so that we might die to sins and live for righteousness; "by his wounds you have been healed" (1 Peter 2:24 NIV).

The phrase "By His stripes we are healed" refers to the punishment Jesus Christ suffered—floggings and beatings followed by His agonizing death on a cross—to take upon Himself all the sins of the world. The sacrifice of Jesus on the cross was the judgment of sin that was due to humanity for their sins. Each of us would have received what is due us for the sins we committed, but Jesus took our place. He took on our punishments, sins, and diseases, freeing us from judgment and punishment.

Due to Christ's great sacrifice, all people who believe in Him as Saviour can step into the freedom Jesus paid for with His blood. Sadly, whoever rejects the sacrifice of Christ ignorantly remains in bondage to Satan, even though Christ purchased their freedom. Each person is presented with Christ and must decide: Christ or the world? Sin or holiness? Bondage to Satan or freedom in Christ? Accept Christ's sacrifice or take on judgment themselves? Sadly, not all people will come to Christ. Many people reject God despite proof of His existence, not because there is no proof, but because they love sin.

Therefore, Jesus says, *"You will die in your sins; for if you do not believe that I am He, you will die in your sins" (John 8:24 NKJV).*

Jesus is the only option for salvation. Those who reject Him cannot get saved. To turn your back on Christ is to turn your back on God Himself. Therefore, those who reject Jesus will die in their sins. Jesus said, *"Most assuredly, I say to you, unless one is born again, he cannot see the kingdom of God" (John 3:3 NKJV).*

A person cannot be redeemed unless he is born again. Jesus was not speaking of a physical rebirth, for it is biologically impossible to be born again physically. Jesus was referring to spiritual birth. In other words, to be born again is to be born from above. A person cannot be redeemed unless he is born again of God. The pain suffered by Jesus on the cross produces rebirth and change in those who turn to Him for salvation, giving them new life in Himself. Those who have been born again are born, not of perishable seed, but of imperishable seed, through the living Word of God – Jesus Christ.

"Having been born again, not of corruptible seed but incorruptible, through the word of God which lives and abides forever" (1 Peter 1:23 NKJV).

Being born physically does not make us alive spiritually. In this life, when we are physically born, we are already dead in sin, due to the corruptible seed of man. But because the new birth springs from an undying seed – Christ Himself – we became spiritually alive forever in Christ. God is the One who makes us alive when we come to Him through faith in Christ. Then we are born again; thus, we become new.

"Therefore, if anyone is in Christ, he is a new creation; old things have passed away; behold, all things have become new" (2 Corinthians 5:17 NKJV).

When you come to Christ, the old version of you has gone. Sins get forgiven, sickness leaves, bondages loosen, witchcraft gets broken, etc. And the new version of you is born, and you are in the image of Christ: free, cleansed, blessed. Reader, the choice is yours. Do you want Jesus in your life? Are you willing to let go of the past? Do you want to change? Will you surrender? Do you believe the message of the cross? Are you ready to walk in the message of the cross? God has given you free will to choose. Choose wisely.

I encourage you to reject everything and surrender to the message of the cross. Let Christ set you free today. Now for the people who have already chosen Christ, you must walk fully and freely in the message of the cross. Otherwise, if Satan seduces you into thinking that you are still that old sinner, that old addict, that corrupt person, then he can hinder your walk in the freedom that Jesus died for. One of the main ways Satan paralyzes a Christian is by associating that person's mind with the old sinful nature, creating guilt and unworthiness, and slowly deforming their mind to make them ineffective. Note that when we carry guilt and the consciousness of sin, we will not have faith to stand before God, let alone live the message of the cross.

Reader, you must believe and walk in the message of the cross – no exception. When you accept Jesus as your personal Saviour, you are a new creation; the old has gone, and the new is here. From that moment on, with the help of the Holy Spirit, you start growing in your walk with God. Don't allow the enemy to tell you anything different. Step out of the deceptive thoughts of lies, sin consciousness, and slave mentality, and step into the reality of Christ that is a new creation in truth and freedom.

Know that the blood shed by Jesus redeems you, and you are spiritually rebirthed because of the blood. You are cleansed, protected, and kept under the blood. Demons and Satan shudder and run because of the blood. God has given you the power to overcome sin by the blood, which has ushered you into life in the Spirit.

Jesus did His part on the cross. Now it's time for you to do your part:

1. Bring all corrupt thoughts under the message of the cross, surrender everything, laying it all down at the cross, and walking in the message of the cross.
2. Let Jesus come in, and let the Holy Spirit lead you into all truth and freedom. Let Jesus help you walk with Him.

The faster you surrender, the quicker you can walk in the freedom that Jesus paid the price for with His blood. As you continue to live by faith with the consciousness of righteousness in Christ, you will soon start manifesting Christ. The faster you surrender, the sooner you will come to a place where you have no more consciousness of sin.

If you haven't already done so, I encourage you to receive Jesus into your life. Let me lead you step-by-step on how to call on the Name of Jesus Christ and be saved. Note that it must be an attitude of the heart that wants to give your life to Christ, not mere spoken words. You must want Him to come into your heart and change you. Are you ready? Let's begin! Wholeheartedly read the following aloud:

"Jesus Christ, I believe You are the Son of God; I believe You died on the cross for my sins, and I believe God raised You from the dead, and that you are alive. I therefore, welcome You into my heart as my Lord and Saviour. Please come to live in me and change me from the inside out.

Jesus Christ, please forgive me of any sins I have ever committed. I regret and repent for my old sinful life. I am sorry that I did not know better. Jesus, I confess my sins, and I ask Your forgiveness, and I receive that forgiveness right now. Jesus, I thank you for breaking the power of sin from me.

Jesus Christ, I now start my new life with You. I ask You to purify, heal, lead, and fill me with Your Holy Spirit. Jesus, I speak this in Your Mighty Name. Amen."

Hallelujah! Beloved reader, welcome to the spiritual family of God the Father. Receive my prayer for you:

"Father in heaven, release Your healing over the person reading this book. In Jesus's name I command all evil influences to leave, I break sinful bondages, I cast down corrupt imaginations, and I ask that You rebuild the reader into the wholeness of Christ. Come into my readers' homes and lives and flood them with love, peace, and gentleness. Fill them with Your Holy Spirit, and give them knowledge, understanding, and wisdom to walk rightly by You from now onward. Father, I pray that Your love, hope, joy, and peace will flow through the reader. I pray that Your light will shine through them to others, bringing healing and deliverance to the reader and those around them. Bathe them in the glorious light of Your love, reflecting Your light in this darkened world and permitting Your love to flow through them to others until You become everything in the readers' life. In the Name of Jesus Christ, I pray. Amen."

THE KINGDOM OF GOD

When Jesus walked the earth, He came preaching and teaching a message directly from God: "The Kingdom of God is at hand." It was the central theme of Jesus's message. He did not come to talk about Himself. The heart of His message was the Kingdom of God. Sadly, many Christians today talk about Jesus without talking about the message He taught. But if the Kingdom of God was at the heart of Jesus's teaching, then we must have it at the heart of our lives. Note that when Jesus healed people, He said, "The Kingdom has come near you."

"Heal the sick who are there and tell them, 'The kingdom of God has come near to you'" (Luke 10:9 NKJV).

What does it mean that the Kingdom of God has come near? Well, a kingdom is where a king rules, and Jesus is the King of God's Kingdom.

"And He has on His robe and on His thigh a name written: KING OF KINGS AND LORD OF LORDS" (Revelation 19:16 NKJV).

When we accept Jesus, the King, into our hearts, He will come and establish His Kingdom in our hearts. That is to say, the Kingdom of God is a dwelling place where Christ resides in all who recognize His sovereignty. Sadly, for those who reject Christ's reign, His Kingdom has not yet come. Therefore, God's Kingdom is yet to get established in such a person.

When the disciples of Jesus went out preaching the Kingdom, they were preparing the hearts of man for Jesus to come and establish His Kingdom. And when Jesus was preaching that the Kingdom is at hand, He was saying, "Come to be set free." Jesus tells us we don't have to experience family strife, addiction, anger, conflict, or any form of bondage. Jesus is stating His Kingdom is here for us to encounter freedom right now.

Understand that Jesus is among believers, which means the Kingdom of God is among believers. The Kingdom is already here and is currently getting set up in the hearts of believers; thus, manifesting on earth through believers. Mankind must only come to Jesus, and then Jesus Himself will free us from darkness's dominion.

Reader, God is calling you today. The Kingdom of God has come near you, and you need only accept Jesus and let his Kingdom begin to be established within you. Allow Him to live in you now, creating in you everything God wants you to be, establishing His Kingdom in you, making you a blessing to your family and those around you. Those willing to come under Christ's rule will inherit the Kingdom of God under the reign of King Jesus.

But please consider this: believing the message of the cross and living the message of the cross are two different things. In other words, to produce the reality of Christ in your life, you must both believe and live in the message of the cross. Allow me to explain. The Kingdom of God is like a seed that must get planted in good soil before it can produce the reality of Jesus Christ, the King of the Kingdom.

"The Kingdom of God is as if a man should scatter seed on the ground, and should sleep by night and rise by day, and the seed should sprout and grow, he himself does not know how. For the earth yields crops by itself: first the blade, then the head, after that the full grain in the head. But when the grain ripens, immediately he puts in the sickle, because the harvest has come" (Mark 4:26-29 NKJV).

Let me explain: the Kingdom of God is the message of the gospel (seed) planted in the hearts of man (ground) that it may produce God's Kingdom (the reality of Jesus Christ in man).

There are three aspects here:

1) The Kingdom of God (which is the reality of Christ)
2) The sower (that is, he who spreads the message of the gospel)
3) The ground (which is the heart of man)

Let's investigate each one individually.

The Kingdom of God
God's Kingdom is any place, situation, or moment where the sovereignty and power of God are recognized—that is, wherever God's Kingdom (the reality of Christ) is present.

The Sower
A sower spreads the gospel's message—that is, to scatter seed.

The Soil
The soil in which the sower sows is the heart of man—that is, a heart that hears the message of the gospel and either orientates toward God or rejects and moves away from God.

Good soil is the heart of a man who accepts the gospel's message, allowing the Word of God to change his life. It is a heart that seeks Jesus wholeheartedly, making Jesus a priority. Such people do not squeeze Jesus into their schedule, but prioritize time for Him. It is a heart that pursues a personal relationship with God, getting to know Him, trusting Him, speaking to Him often, and treating Him with love and respect. For such people, God is the highest priority. They hunger and thirst for God. They receive Jesus into their hearts as the Messiah and participate in the Kingdom He is establishing. Thus, they produce good crops (the spiritual reality of Christ), bringing forth Kingdom fruit: joy, love, peace, gentleness, healing, deliverance, etc. In such people, Jesus spills over into every aspect of their life. That's how to produce the reality of Jesus Christ.

Contrary to good soil is the heart of any man that rejects the gospel's message. Such people have deaf ears to the message of God. Others may get excited about Jesus, but then it becomes a chore; they let other things get in the way, leaving no time for God. Their weak faith crumbles when tested by the troubles of life. They get consumed by worldly worries and are drawn away by worldly goals: wealth, beauty, status, etc. Thus, the seed sown into their hearts fails to produce fruitful plants (no spiritual reality of Christ). In such people, the Kingdom of God has not yet come.

Then we have lukewarm Christians. They are the people who have accepted Christ, are born again, and have the Holy Spirit in them, but are not dedicated fully to God. They love Jesus, they speak of Jesus, and read the Bible, but have not laid their lives down for His Kingdom to manifest. They lack complete surrender. They are spiritually lazy.

Reader, which soil are you like? What is the attitude of your heart toward Christ? Has the Kingdom of God come to you? Understand that Scripture is a bag full of seeds that we, believers, must sow into our hearts and into the hearts of others before we can see spiritual fruit. We must work together with God for this to come about.

For this reason, the Bible says, *"We are God's fellow workers" (1 Corinthians 3:9 NKJV).*

In other words, you must co-work with God before you can experience the reality of Christ. God doesn't give you the apple tree but the apple seed. Then you must sow the seed and water it before you can harvest Christ's reality. The reality of Christ is healing, peace, joy, love, gentleness, patience, goodness, and more. And you have the seed to those things. Everything that God wants to give you in the Kingdom, He gives you in the form of seeds, not fruit. Your job is to co-work with God to sow, water, and harvest those spiritual fruits.

Between sowing the seed and harvest there is a growing season, which can be painful and uncomfortable. There may be afflictions or trials during this season. Your job as a follower of Christ is to hold onto that seed (Word of God) so that it produces manifold fruit, making you fruitful in the Kingdom of God. That's when you produce the spiritual reality of Christ, manifesting God's Kingdom everywhere you go.

Reader, are you beginning to understand how important it is to sow and water before you can produce Christ's reality? You must co-work with God to bring Kingdom seed to fruition so that there can be a physical manifestation of God's heaven on earth. Then, as faithful followers of Christ, we are to feed those spiritual fruits to those living in sin and darkness so that they may come alive in Christ– that's how to invade and destroy Satan's darkness while simultaneously manifesting God's Kingdom on earth.

But note that it all begins with a union with Christ. The manifestation of Christ's Kingdom on earth is a product of a relationship with Christ. To produce the reality of Christ with more ease, we must mature into the likeness of Christ. We do this by constantly practicing the experience of God. We do this by sitting in the presence of God, making Him our constant state of mind.

It helps to become childlike. I am not referring to childish foolishness, but childlike maturity. For example, just as children pretend to be this or that character, absorbed into the role they play; likewise as a follower of Christ you must mature into childlikeness, soaking in Christ as you practice experiencing God. Start by sitting in the presence of God, walking in His likeness, and making Him your constant state of mind. Childlikeness means you need God: you turn to God, depend on Him, and need Him as a child needs his parent. You must bond with God until He becomes your all.

Jesus said, *"Unless you are converted and become as little children, you will by no means enter the kingdom of heaven" (Matthew 18:3 NKJV)*.

Childlikeness is an attitude of the heart that shapes you into the likeness of Christ. It's about recognizing that you are entirely dependent on God, powerless without Him, and that you need Him to provide for you and protect you. Only with this kind of childlikeness can the reality of Christ produce in you, establishing His Kingdom with each passing day.

Let's take Jesus, for example, He turned to the Father for everything. Thus, the Father was able to work signs and wonders through Jesus. And we must follow the examples of Jesus. Be childlike; go and sit with God and make peace with Him. Talk with Him, magnify Him, and glorify Him. Look at Him as a baby looks at his mother and depends upon her for everything. Practice engaging with His presence until His presence becomes tangible and real. With enough practice, you establish God's Kingdom in you, and you will be spiritually fruitful. Even the storms of life won't move you when you walk in the consciousness of God's Kingdom.

YOUR INHERITANCE IN CHRIST

"Of the increase of His government and peace there will be no end, upon the throne of David and over His kingdom, to order it and establish it with judgment and justice from that time forward, even forever" (Isaiah 9:7 NKJV).

Government is not a metaphor – Christ was born to rule. He will rule the world, and His manifested Kingdom on earth will have no end. The followers of Jesus will also rule under Christ when the time comes for His Kingdom to cover the whole earth.

"The saints of the Most High shall receive the kingdom, and possess the kingdom forever, even forever and ever" (Daniel 7:18 NKJV).

We (followers of Christ) shall rule and govern the whole world under Jesus Christ. We will reign on the earth with Him.

"And have made us kings and priests to our God; and we shall reign on the earth" (Revelation 5:10 NKJV).

Jesus has made all the redeemed a Kingdom and priests. The Lord promises the conquerors (believers) who hold fast through faith will share His throne. Believers will be given power and dominion to reign on the earth.

"And he who overcomes, and keeps My works until the end, to him I will give power over the nations" (Revelation 2:26 NKJV).

A time is coming when God's Kingdom will rule the earth. All who stand firm with Christ will get granted a position of authority over the nations, giving them the privilege of sharing in His rule. That is part of the inheritance that believers have in Christ.

"Blessed be the God and Father of our Lord Jesus Christ, who according to His abundant mercy has begotten us again to a living hope through the resurrection of Jesus Christ from the dead, to an

inheritance incorruptible and undefiled and that does not fade away, reserved in heaven for you" (1 Peter 1:3-4 NKJV).

Believers have been born again into an inheritance that can never perish, spoil, or fade. This inheritance is in heaven waiting for us. Our inheritance is imperishable. It is not subject to corruption or decay. Unlike everything on earth that is decaying, rusting, or falling apart, our treasure in heaven is unaffected by corrosion and deterioration. Furthermore, our inheritance is also to sit with Christ in the heavenly realm.

"God, who is rich in mercy, because of His great love with which He loved us, even when we were dead in trespasses, made us alive together with Christ (by grace you have been saved), and raised us up together, and made us sit together in the heavenly places in Christ Jesus" (Ephesians 2:4-6 NKJV).

Followers are spiritually seated in the heavens with Christ. In other words, we live up there but function down here. We have a heavenly perspective while our feet stand firmly on the ground. We get our data from heaven while we faithfully walk the earth. In other words, we do everything from the perspective of heavens, not earth's worldview.

In addition to everything mentioned, our inheritance is unspoiled. What we have in Christ is free from anything that would deform, debase, or degrade. Everything in this world is flawed and imperfect, but our inheritance in Him is holy, blameless, and pure. No earthly corruption nor weakness can touch what God has bestowed.

"But there shall by no means enter it anything that defiles, or causes an abomination or a lie, but only those who are written in the Lamb's Book of Life" (Revelation 21:27 NKJV).

Nothing impure will ever enter God's Kingdom, nor will anyone who does what is shameful or deceitful.

In addition, our inheritance is unfading. Everything in this world fades away, dies, and depreciates, but our inheritance is not of this world. Its glorious intensity will never diminish.

In addition, our inheritance has been reserved. What we have in Christ is being kept in heaven for us. Although we enjoy many blessings as children of God here on earth, our true inheritance—our true home—is reserved for us in heaven. The Holy Spirit guarantees that we will receive eternal life in the world to come. As God's children, adopted into His family, we have been assured an inheritance from our Heavenly Father.

"And if children, then heirs—heirs of God and joint heirs with Christ, if indeed we suffer with Him, that we may also be glorified together" (Romans 8:17 NKJV).

God has made everyone who trusts in Christ an heir to all the glory of God's Kingdom. If we suffer with Christ in manifesting God's Kingdom on earth, we are heirs to Christ. One day, we will take possession of our full heritage, where the river of life will issue from God's throne.

"And he showed me a pure river of water of life, clear as crystal, proceeding from the throne of God and of the Lamb. In the middle of its street, and on either side of the river, was the tree of life, which bore twelve fruits, each tree yielding its fruit every month. The leaves of the tree were for the healing of the nations" (Revelation 22:1-2 NKJV).

The water flowing from the throne of God is symbolic of the water of eternal life, crystal clear to reflect the glory of God in a dazzling, never-ending stream. The fact that the stream emanates from the throne tells us that eternal life flows from God to His people.

"Therefore with joy you will draw water from the wells of salvation" (Isaiah 12:3 NKJV).

Just as physical water is necessary to sustain physical life on earth, living water from our Saviour is needed to maintain eternal life. Jesus is the source of living water, sustaining His people forever. Reader, when we understand and value the glory that awaits us, we can better endure whatever comes our way. We can praise God even during trials because we have His guarantee that we will receive all He has promised. Sadly, people forsake the living God, who provides eternal life, to chase after false idols, worldliness, and works-based religions. Worldwide, people refuse the water of life, that only Christ can provide, for a parched and dusty life of materialism and self-indulgence. But this kind of living cannot get you eternal life with Jesus.

GOD IS LOOKING FOR COMMITTED VESSELS

God is looking for people who will commit their lives to Him in complete trust and confidence so that they may go out into the world, bringing His Kingdom to the hearts of man, and manifesting God's Kingdom on earth. At the same time, they are invading and destroying the kingdom of darkness that is in the world.

God always had a select few throughout history that were committed to Him: Abraham, Daniel, Moses, Elijah, etc. God is still looking for a body of people today. Reader, you can be part of that select few by surrendering to God's will for your life, allowing His Kingdom to be established within you, that you may then go out into the world and advance His Kingdom on earth. That is the job of the church – the body of Christ.

Neither churches nor individuals should not get defeated by evil works, for believers have the power and authority over the devil to go out into the world and set all captives free. The church of Christ must wake up, arise, and take its victorious position in Christ.

Jesus told us that we will not only do the great works He did but even more wondrous works we will do. Jesus destroyed the powers of darkness in the spiritual realm, but now we (vessels of God) must manifest that reality (God's Kingdom) on earth. Although we know that Jesus defeated the enemy at Calvary, evil works still occur in our land because people give the enemy ground. Fortunately, Jesus gave us, the anointed children of God, the power to walk and tread on serpents and destroy the works of the enemy on earth, manifesting God's Kingdom as we invade the darkness.

That's the job of the church – the body of Christ. The church does not exist for heaven but for the earth. God doesn't need a church in heaven. He needs it on earth. God doesn't need pastors and teachers in heaven. He needs them on earth. He doesn't need a prophet in heaven saying, "The Lord said..." He doesn't need an evangelist in heaven because in heaven no one needs to get saved there. The church exists for the earth, not for heaven. Therefore, it is the job of the church to manifest God's Kingdom on earth as it is in heaven.

"Your Kingdom come. Your will be done on earth as it is in heaven" (Matthew 6:10 NKJV).

We, the church, are to manifest God amid a lost and dying world. We must step out in God's power and cast down the high places, darkness, and wickedness. Reader, this is done by executing God's power and authority wherever there is darkness. That's how to bring His heaven to earth.

The church must come together as a corporate body with the power and authority imparted to her by Christ, then go out into the world, manifesting God's heaven, influencing places, and possessing the land. The church must dominate the whole world!

Jesus penetrated the kingdom of darkness with His light. He began to transform what He saw as a dark, desolate planet and people. We must do the same. We must continue the ministry of Christ.

It's time for the church to advance the Kingdom of God into this world, into families, and into workplaces. We must invade the darkness, and fill people and places with the light of the gospel. We are to preach the gospel to change societies, cultures, etc. But the church cannot influence if she is hiding.

"You are the light of the world. A city that is set on a hill cannot be hidden. Nor do they light a lamp and put it under a basket, but on a lampstand, and it gives light to all who are in the house. Let your light so shine before men, that they may see your good works and glorify your Father in heaven" (Matthew 5:14-16 NKJV).

It's time for the church to stand up and walk as Christ has called us. When we live by God's ways, He gives us dominion to bring order into the chaos and light into the darkness. It's time to take authority. Jesus commanded us to go and make disciples.

"Go therefore and make disciples of all the nations, baptizing them in the name of the Father and of the Son and of the Holy Spirit, teaching them to observe all things that I have commanded you; and lo, I am with you always, even to the end of the age." (Matthew 28:19-20 NKJV).

We are to make followers of Jesus, advancing His Kingdom, bringing Kingdom life, Kingdom principles, and the gospel of the Kingdom to the ends of the earth, thus, bringing order into the chaos and light into the darkness.

"I, therefore, the prisoner of the Lord, beseech you to walk worthy of the calling with which you were called, with all lowliness and gentleness, with longsuffering, bearing with one another in love, endeavoring to keep the unity of the Spirit in the bond of peace. There is one body and one Spirit, just as you were called in one hope of your calling; one Lord, one faith, one baptism; one God and Father of all, who is above all, and through all, and in you all" (Ephesians 4:1-6 NKJV)

THE CHOICE OF LIFE OR DEATH

Every man and woman want happiness; they *wish to obtain life and goodness and to escape death and evil;* they desire happiness and dread misery. And they will go to any lengths to get happiness. I inform you that God is the giver of eternal life, of goodness, and of happiness; but to attain these things you must choose Him and His ways. To choose God's ways is the best decision one can make. God's commandments are not beyond our ability; they are easily understood and not too difficult to obey.

"For this commandment which I command you today is not too mysterious for you, nor is it far off. It is not in heaven, that you should say, 'Who will ascend into heaven for us and bring it to us, that we may hear it and do it?' Nor is it beyond the sea, that you should say, 'Who will go over the sea for us and bring it to us, that we may hear it and do it?' But the word is very near you, in your mouth and in your heart, that you may do it. See, I have set before you today life and good, death and evil, in that I command you today to love the Lord your God, to walk in His ways, and to keep His commandments, His statutes, and His judgments, that you may live and multiply; and the Lord your God will bless you in the land which you go to possess. But if your heart turns away so that you do not hear, and are drawn away, and worship other gods and serve them, I announce to you today that you shall surely perish; you shall not prolong your days in the land which you cross over the Jordan to go in and possess. I call heaven and earth as witnesses today against you, that I have set before you life and death, blessing and cursing; therefore choose life, that both you and your descendants may live; that you may love the Lord your God, that you may obey His voice, and that you may cling to Him, for He is your life and the length of your days; and that you may dwell in the land which the Lord swore to your fathers, to Abraham, Isaac, and Jacob, to give them" (Deuteronomy 30:11-20 NKJV).

There are two roads in life. One is good, and the other is evil; one leads to life, and the other to death. Every day you have a choice to believe God or the devil, to follow God or the devil. God said to

Adam and Eve, "If you eat of the fruit, you will surely die." Satan said, "You surely won't die." God said, "Don't eat of that tree." Satan said, "Go and eat it." Then Adam and Eve had a choice: to believe and obey God or Satan. To obey God is life; to obey Satan is death. Obedience to God leads to prosperity and life, and disobedience leads to adversity and death.

Man gets to choose if he wants to obey God or not. God does not force anyone to live the good and righteous life. God lets us make our choice; otherwise, without free will He would deprive us of our capacity to choose. God does not want the automatic, mechanical responses of robots. He wants a purposeful, loving relationship with us. He wants meaningful responses of love, which require choice and free will. He gives us the capacity to choose a relationship with Him. If you decide you want a relationship with God, you will have it. But if you are evil, you will not want a relationship with Him; for He requires that you repent of your evil and believe in His Son. Jesus said that those who refused to come to Him did so because they were evil and didn't want their evil deeds exposed in His light.

Reader, today I set two options before you that you may choose: Life or death? Good or evil? Understand that it is not a multiple choice; it is one or the other. Your whole life is a matter of choice.

Understand that God is good and wants to bless you with health and happiness, with affluence of all good things. Still, if your heart turns away from Him and His commands, so that you do not obey Him but get drawn away by an evil heart and the ill examples of others, then you shall perish.

"The soul who sins shall die" (Ezekiel 18:20 NKJV).

I call you to love God and have no other gods nor priorities before Him. Let your love for Him exceed every other love in your life. No other love must compete. Establish a relationship with the Lord by committing yourself wholly to Him and His ways. Love and trust Him by obeying His voice, and show it by keeping His commands; for a child who loves and trusts his Father will abide by Him. Turn your heart to God, pray, read your Bible, go to church, listen to His warnings, cleave to Him, and worship His holy Name. Believe and apply His ways, speak His Word through confession, faithfully keep it, cheerfully submit to it, be not ashamed of it, and profess it before man.

God's statutes are correct and will cause your heart to rejoice. His commandments are pure and will enlighten your eyes. And in the keeping of them, there is great reward. God will bless you. You will have life, favor, and prosperity. You will see His hand of blessing and protection in your life – this is grace. The question is will you choose God?

Jesus said to His Father, *"Not My will, but Yours, be done" (Luke 22:42 NKJV).*

Reader, I encourage you to strive toward holiness with God. Direct yourself and your time and energies toward fellowship with God. Aim to please Him. Decide now that when you close your eyes for the last time, you will have made Jesus proud. Sign the contract today that you will do life in Jesus Christ. Reader, that's my Christian walk with God. I choose to dwell with the King.

"One thing I have desired of the Lord, that will I seek: that I may dwell in the house of the Lord all the days of my life, to behold the beauty of the Lord, and to inquire in His temple. For in the time of trouble He shall hide me in His pavilion; in the secret place of His tabernacle He shall hide me; He shall set me high upon a rock. And now my head shall be lifted up above my enemies all around me; therefore I will offer sacrifices of joy in His tabernacle; I will sing, yes, I will sing praises to the Lord" (Psalm 27:4-6 NKJV).

Reader, my own heart seeks the beauty of God. I long for His presence and yearn to spend the rest of my life in worship. The love is mutual, for God desires to bring me into His dwelling place and secretly hide me there. In life, I want nothing more than God's presence. It's my protection where I feel safe. My enemies cannot reach me there. Therefore, I refuse to get tempted to faint under persecution; instead, I choose to cling to faith without wavering. I am confident that I am safe in Christ, who tabernacles within me. He gives me eternal life; I will never perish, and no one will snatch me out of His hand. Our chief enemy, the devil, would love to snatch me from my Saviour's hand and destroy me, but this will never happen.

The Lord Jesus promised to be with me always, even to the end of the age. He will never leave me nor forsake me. Knowing that the Lord is present with me always and everywhere, I rejoice significantly with thanksgiving. It is this truth that I cling to when circumstances cause anxiety.

"As for me and my house, we will serve the Lord" (Joshua 24:15 NKJV).

        The peace of our Lord, Jesus Christ, be with you.

ABOUT INFO

More Books by Venetia:

Who is God
New Age Occult to Jesus Christ
Worldly Life of Deception
Spiritual Warfare

Email: Venetia.VenetiaZ@gmail.com
Social Media: Venetia Zannettis Ministries
Donations: linktr.ee/VenetiaZannettis

Printed in Poland
by Amazon Fulfillment
Poland Sp. z o.o., Wrocław